THE
TEMPTATION
TO DO GOOD

Books by Peter F. Drucker

THE TEMPTATION TO DO GOOD

THE LAST OF ALL POSSIBLE WORLDS

THE CHANGING WORLD OF THE EXECUTIVE

TOWARD THE NEXT ECONOMICS

MANAGING IN TURBULENT TIMES

ADVENTURES OF A BYSTANDER

THE UNSEEN REVOLUTION

MANAGEMENT: TASKS, RESPONSIBILITIES, PRACTICES

MEN, IDEAS, AND POLITICS

TECHNOLOGY, MANAGEMENT, AND SOCIETY

THE AGE OF DISCONTINUITY

THE EFFECTIVE EXECUTIVE

MANAGING FOR RESULTS

LANDMARKS OF TOMORROW

AMERICA'S NEXT TWENTY YEARS

THE PRACTICE OF MANAGEMENT

THE NEW SOCIETY

CONCEPT OF THE CORPORATION

THE FUTURE OF INDUSTRIAL MAN

THE END OF ECONOMIC MAN

THE
TEMPTATION TO DO GOOD

PETER F. DRUCKER

1817

HARPER & ROW, PUBLISHERS, New York
Cambridge, Philadelphia, San Francisco, London
Mexico City, São Paulo, Sydney

FIRST EDITION

Designer: C. Linda Dingler

Library of Congress Cataloging in Publication Data

Drucker, Peter Ferdinand, 1909–
  The temptation to do good.

  I. Title.
PS3554.R7T4 1984   813'.54   83-48341
ISBN 0-06-015253-2

84 85 86 87 88 10 9 8 7 6 5 4 3 2 1

PART ONE

That something was very wrong she knew the moment she saw the mail, still neatly bundled, lying on the floor outside the unopened office door.

She had the key, of course; often she was the first to get to the office, but only when Father President was either sick or out of town. And he had been perfectly well and hadn't said a word about a trip or an early-morning appointment yesterday, Sunday, when she had taken him the folders on several potential donors to the university he wanted to work on, and he asked her to stay and have lunch with him, Father Ritter, and Dr. Meyeroff, the new Law School dean.

No, Father Heinz was not out of town and not sick—and yet he wasn't there ahead of her. Nothing like this had ever happened before. She found herself trembling with anxiety as she stooped to pick up the mail and then fumbled for the key to the door.

She half expected to hear, as on every normal morning, his light baritone singing out: "Agnes, good morning, come in and help me sort the mail." But everything was emptiness and silence in the president's office.

She was so shaky that she had to sit down at her desk, still in her coat and the heavy gloves and fur hat she had put on to protect herself against the icy winds of a January cold wave during the walk from her little house, just outside the campus gates, first to hear Mass at the chapel of St. Mary in the Plains, and then across the sprawling campus to her own office.

She knew she was silly and superstitious. Surely nothing

whatever could be the matter. Father Heinz had overslept, or had been delayed by an early telephone call—in the East, in New York and Washington, the business day, after all, was already in full swing—or a dean or department head had waylaid him on the way from saying Mass at the university church.

But while she knew in her mind that there was nothing to worry about, she was filled with a dread she could not shake off. She had not been so frightened since the day they had phoned her and told her: "Jake has had an accident"—and she had known at once that her husband was dead.

In the secretarial course at St. Mary in the Plains Girls' High School, from which she had graduated first in her class, she had been taught that the proper secretary always arrives at the office ahead of her boss. And Sister Hildegard, the assistant principal of the school, who had hired her before she even graduated, had made it very clear that she expected her secretary to be at her desk and ready for the day's work when she herself showed up at eight. So when, twenty years ago now, she first began to work for Father Zimmerman (even then, of course, everybody else was calling him Father Heinz, if not simply Heinz), she had made carefully sure of getting to the office fifteen minutes earlier than he. Yet she soon sensed that this irritated him—he wanted to be alone with the mail. He never said a word; but three or four weeks into the job, when she had asked him, "Would you rather have me come in a little later?" a smile of total relief lit up his face and he happily nodded assent. So she scheduled herself to arrive exactly twenty minutes later than he did.

It took them only a few months more to develop the daily routine for working together—the routine that had not been changed or broken once until today.

He was a creature of habits, as men who live alone so often are. And she knew his habits, knew them as well as if she had shared a bed with him. He was up every morning at six-thirty, did ten minutes of vigorous exercising, shaved, showered and, at seven sharp, walked over to the university church to say Mass. He liked to linger over Mass—" I abhor priests who apply time and motion study to make the Mass efficient," he had said once, to the great annoyance of that man of efficiency, Bishop O'Malley. But still he was through by 7:45 and, after disrobing, got to his office always a minute or two after 8.

She, too, got up at 6:30. But then she had to make breakfast—for years for the children, now only for her old mother who still lived with her. This delayed her leaving the house until 7:15, just in time for the 7:30 Mass at the Chapel of St. Mary in the Plains and for an 8:20 or 8:25 arrival at the office. And there the door with its frosted glass marked: FATHER HENRY ZIMMERMAN: PH.D.; CSH; PRESIDENT, and below it, in smaller letters: "Mrs. Agnes Muller, Assistant to the President," would already be open and the lights turned on in all four rooms of the president's suite, Father's big corner office, her own outer office, his conference room and her own (much smaller) conference room, one corner of which she had converted into a kitchen and pantry with a gas burner, a cabinet, a small refrigerator, and sink.

Father Heinz would be standing at his big desk, with his back to the window, opening the mail. But before she reached the door, he'd sense her coming and would sing out: "Good morning, Agnes, come in and help me sort the mail." And before she could even hang up her coat, he'd say something flattering or pleasant: "How nice you look this morning," or, "That's a very becoming dress you're wearing today," or, "Come quick—we got a really nice donation in the mail. It's all because you wrote such a skillful begging letter."

Father loved mail—was obsessed by mail. As soon as it came in he threw himself at it, sorted it, and opened every letter, even the sandwich menu from the local deli down the road. "It's a legacy of the war years," he explained once when she told him he'd missed his vocation and should have become a postal clerk. "Whether you're in combat or not, nothing is more boring than to be a soldier—and I had to be one for three long years during World War II. It was almost a relief when I got shot up at Anzio; at least something had finally happened. The one break in that mindless, endless monotony was the mail call: the suspense as to whether your name would be called, the ecstasy when there was a letter for you, no matter who from or what was inside it. They say," he added, "that people who have suffered through a long famine will always wolf down their food no matter how much is on the table. Well, soldiering to me was worse than any famine I can imagine, and lasted longer—and mail was what food is to a starving man. We dreamed of it when we didn't get it and wolfed it down when we did. And I still do."

Then she'd go and get breakfast: strong black coffee and two soft-boiled eggs for Father, with a few slices of the dark heavy German bread she baked for him as she had earlier baked it for Jake, and ample servings of the jams and jellies she put up every summer. They would eat breakfast sitting together at the table in her conference room. During those ten minutes, talk of business was strictly forbidden.

Then they'd move to his office, where they sat across from each other at his big desk, and the day's work would begin. First they'd dispose of the mail. Then they'd tackle the day's agenda, first his appointments and meetings, on which he'd ask her advice; then her work and projects, particularly those where she needed a decision from him. If Father Heinz had to give a speech, especially on something that was a little offbeat, or if he had to make a presentation for funds to a government agency or a foundation, or write an article or one of his annual reports (to Regents, faculty, alumni, or students), she would have roughed out the first draft, which they would then polish together. They also discussed in these morning sessions the approach to donors, after she had first done the research on them and drawn up what Father called a "donor profile."

Then, usually around ten or eleven, they would each start separately on their own working day. Today, for instance, Father had an eleven o'clock appointment in town with a potential donor, a local oil millionaire, whose donor's profile she had done Saturday night at home and brought to his house yesterday before lunch. At 3:30 he had a session with the dean of faculties and the Tenure Committee on the final decisions for next year's tenure appointments. She herself had a 10:30 session—it would last through lunch—in her conference room with the heads of the eleven departments who reported to her: all the university's noninstructional and nonfinancial functions. It was the first round on the budget for the next academic year, 1980–81, and together her departments accounted for half the university's total expenditures.

That had been the routine five or six days every week, for more often than not they would both come to the office on Saturdays, too. And it had remained unchanged, even though both her work and her title had changed. When they first began to work together, Father had only recently been appointed assistant to an ailing president and she, recently widowed, had been hired as a stenotypist and to answer his phone. But just a few months later Father turned over to her two important departments: Personnel and Building and Grounds. "And since then," Agnes Muller said to herself, "I've been in on every one of the big ones: the start-up of the Engineering School, the merger with St. Mary in the Plains Women's College, setting up the Graduate School of Arts and Sciences and the Graduate School of Management, the health-care schools, Dentistry, Pharmacy, and Nursing, and the Advanced Institute of Theoretical Physics, and only last year the expansion of the Law School—all the moves that have converted a cow college in the sticks, known only for its basketball team, the Jerome Lions, into a national university.

"And now Father Heinz is a famous university president. And even though I never went to college and only have a

7

high-school degree in secretarial studies, I sit on the Executive Commitee and Father wanted to make me a vice president when he reorganized the university's top management three years ago.

"I was passionately in love with Jake," she thought, "in all the years of our marriage before he was killed. Yet I don't think I was ever as happy with him those six years as I've been every day in this drab office. It's only two days since I sat across from Father and worked with him at his desk. Is it all over now?

"It's not even nine," the more rational half of her countered. "Why the hysterics? He'll be here any minute now and there'll be a perfectly rational explanation." He came only minutes later, but there was no rational explanation; only worse nightmare.

When he came in, he did indeed say, "Good morning, Agnes," but he didn't stop at her desk, just kept on walking. She proferred him the mail; he pushed it aside, saying "Later." Then he went through the door and closed it behind him—the very first time in twenty years that the door between their offices had been shut. After a minute or two she timidly got up, knocked at his door—something she had never had to do before—and asked, "Shall I make breakfast?"

"No need to," he answered. "I slept poorly and am not hungry. Perhaps a cup of coffee, that would be nice. Can you bring it in to me, please?" And when she had brought it in, he did not ask her to sit down and join him but said instead: "Please close my door and hold all calls. I have some thinking to do." Not even a "Thank you," let alone a question about her, a comment, or any explanation.

She was so overcome that she buried her face in her hands. Something made her look up, however, so that she caught sight of the red light flashing on her switchboard: Father Heinz was making a call. This, too, had never happened before— he had always asked her to put calls through for him and usually wanted her to listen in and make notes. Now he sat behind a closed door and dialed a call, shutting her out entirely.

She was racked by slow, painful sobs. To keep them soundless cost so much effort that she didn't even notice, twenty minutes later, that the light on the switchboard was going on again. Father Heinz was making a second call behind the closed door, without telling her.

Father Heinz Zimmerman, president of St. Jerome University, had turned his chair sideways so that he faced what Agnes Muller called the "trophy wall." In its center hung his proudest possession, the honorary doctorate, its citation in sonorous Latin, awarded him by Freiburg University in Germany where he had gone for his advanced degree, on the twenty-fifth anniversary of what the Germans call "Promotion," his receiving the Doctor of Philosophy degree. Ranged around it like an oval frame were his six honorary doctorates from American universities, with the most prestigious, the one from Columbia in New York City, at the top. And arranged around those in a square were his main civic honors. They consisted of two *Time* magazine covers with his portrait, one from 1965 honoring him as the university president who had increased endowment by the largest proportion in the preceding five years, the other from 1970 featuring him as the university president who had most skillfully handled the student unrest of the late sixties; a presidential citation from Lyndon Johnson for serving on the Civil Rights Commission; the Brotherhood Award from the National Conference of Christians and Jews; and the Certificates of Election to their respective boards from the Medieval Academy of America, the American Association of University Presidents, the Boy Scouts, and the American Red Cross. On either side of these hung photographs of the winning basketball teams on which he had played in his high school and college days.

"Of course, it's pure vanity, and in spades," he'd say to any visitor who looked at the display, as a visitor was supposed to do. "But it reminds me of the good friends and colleagues I have in so many places, who are working in their own way for the same things I believe in and am working for."

Father Heinz (for he rarely thought of himself simply as Heinz and never as Henry) loved to look at the trophy wall. It always reassured him and cheered him up whenever he was upset or angry.

But today the trophy wall was invisible to him; he sat staring sightlessly into space.

"I've been rude to Agnes," he said to himself; "I should have apologized. But I need to be alone and not have anyone around till I've calmed down."

Today, for the first time since his ordination as a priest more than a quarter century ago, he had been unable to concentrate at Mass, and unable to concentrate when he knelt afterwards and tried to find serenity and inner strength in a long prayer. Somehow the memory of the Holloways intruded even when he raised the Cup to his lips.

He had never been a mystic or much interested in the mystic's experiences. His theology professor in Freiburg had made him read the German mystics, Roswitha von Gandersheim, Meister Eckhart, and Jakob Boehme. And on his own he had tackled St. John of the Cross, the great Spaniard. But he had never felt as they felt, shared in their experiences, or even glimpsed the visions that filled them with such exquisite pain and the fire of love. It was surely no accident that he choose for his doctoral dissertation the most rationalist of the Schoolmen, the superb logician and anti-mystic Peter Abélard—sentimental, to be sure, and a teen-age romantic in that celebrated love affair with Héloïse, but icily cold and systematic in his thought, and hostile to anything not susceptible to logical proof. The concluding sentence of his thesis had read: "If Abélard had had Arabic numerals and the tools of algebra at his disposal in the early twelfth century, quantification in logic would have begun then instead of having to wait eight hundred years for Russell and Whitehead in 1900 Cambridge and the Logical Positivists in 1920 Vienna."

But during Mass Heinz Zimmerman did experience for a few minutes each day a taste of that ecstasy in which mystics spend their lives. He savored anew every word each day, willed every gesture, lived the Mass with his whole being: with mind and body, reason and emotions. Today, however, the Mass had failed him—or rather, he had failed the Mass. Today, it had been exercise rather than experience, obligation rather than ecstasy.

"But what is it," Heinz Zimmerman asked himself, "that upsets me so dreadfully? What happened yesterday was nothing out of the ordinary. An imcompetent faculty member and his aggressive wife came to see me to appeal a unanimous decision on the part of the faculty in the field, the chairman of the department, and the dean of faculties not to renew the man's contract. They surely knew that I have no control over such a decision. What's more, the decision was fully justified, indeed, the only possible one on the record.

"That the Holloways are upset and angry I can understand, even though we warned him when we hired him three years ago that it was a probationary appointment, not on the tenure track, and that the probability of his being reappointed wasn't great. But why am *I* so upset? Things like this have happened countless times before without causing me more than five minutes of concern."

Sunday had started out pleasant and relaxed. In the morning, after Mass, he had played tennis for two hours on the university's new indoor courts, and had beaten the faculty's best player, a man twenty years his junior. Dick Meyeroff of the Law School had come for lunch and greatly impressed them all—himself and Erwin Ritter, and Agnes, who had brought some work and stayed for the meal—with his first report since he had taken over as dean the preceding fall.

"I've analyzed the Bar examination records of our graduates," Meyeroff had started, "and found that the decline in their scores to where fewer than seventy-five percent now pass the first time around—the decline that rightly concerned you so much, Father Heinz, when you made me dean of the Law School five months ago—is concentrated in two fields. They are the fields which ironically, but not perhaps surprisingly, are being taught by the two most eminent legal scholars on our faculty. I am arranging for our best assistant professors to take the cram sessions in these two subjects, and have instructed them to stress practice rather than history or theory. I think you'll see a decided change in the Bar examination results as early as this summer.

"And then I've appointed a competent placement officer to help our graduates get a decent first job with a good law firm or a good clerkship in the courts. Our top graduates place themselves; the others need help. And I'm proposing to the Law School faculty that twice a year we run a Practicing Law Institute of three weeks' duration, for which our third-year students will serve as staff. This way they'll see what the practice of law is all about, and also get to be known by prospective employers."

Meyeroff's appointment as dean of the Law School had been a break with tradition, opposed by the old-timers, and especially by Erwin Ritter, dean of faculties and Heinz Zimmerman's oldest friend at St. Jerome. The Law School dean had always before been a priest, a St. Jerome graduate, and a canon lawyer. Meyeroff was a tax expert, a product of Chicago who had come to St. Jerome only six years earlier, and, of course, no Catholic. But when he left after lunch, Ritter said: "I've got to admit it, Heinz. I was wrong and you were right. He's exactly what the Law School needs."

Then Heinz Zimmerman had settled down to a few hours' work on the donor profiles Agnes had brought over.

But it was only three, though quite dark—for it was a midwinter day with snow falling steadily since morning—when Erwin Ritter had come into his study. "Sorry to interrupt you,

Father President," and the formal salutation gave warning of something both official and unpleasant, "but Professor and Mrs. Holloway would like a few minutes of your time."

He would not, of course, have recognized them, even though Professor Holloway's appearance was eye-catching: a tall, cadaverous scarecrow with eyes set deep in the long bony face, an untidy shock of bright red hair, and clothes that seemed to have been made for a man two sizes heavier. But there were now almost a thousand faculty members at St. Jerome, eight times what the faculty had been in his own student days thirty-five years ago. And he surely had never met the wife, a dumpy woman dressed in crumpled tweeds.

But he recognized the name immediately and knew at once why they had come, and also why they had done so without telephoning ahead for an appointment.

He had first heard of Holloway three years earlier when Erwin Ritter and Clem Boglund, the chairman of chemistry, had come to consult him. "We wouldn't have bothered you, Heinz," Ritter had said, "but for the memo you sent to all of us a few weeks ago warning against discrimination by age in faculty appointments. Among the applicants for a starting position in Chemistry is a Martin Holloway, a doctoral candidate at Purdue. His adviser there—Clem's known him for years and trusts him—tells us that he'll have his thesis finished this term and recommends him as conscientious. He had fifteen years' experience working in industry before he went back for his Ph.D.—and that's a plus Clem thinks, as the students need a whiff of the practical. But he's almost forty-four. If we hire him now for his first probationary appointment and he doesn't work out (and two out of three don't, as you know), he'll be forty-seven and way too old to get another teaching job. Personally," Ritter had finished, "I wouldn't hire anyone that old for the entrance job. But in view of your memo, Clem and I thought we should consult you."

"Is his age the main reason you wouldn't hire him?" Zimmerman had asked; and when Ritter nodded, he said: "Then I have no choice but to order you to hire him. Anything else is a clear violation of the law. But make sure you spell out in your letter to him that the odds for reappointment three years hence are quite poor and that it will depend on his publications and on the semi-annual appraisals of his teaching performance. And Clem," he had added, "the appraisals better be very thorough. I suggest you do them yourself and make sure they are read and signed by Holloway and are clearly recorded."

And now, only three weeks ago, right after the New Year, Ritter and Boglund had come into his office with a unanimous recommendation from the tenured Chemistry faculty not to reappoint Holloway, in which the chairman of the department had fully concurred.

"We have no alternative," Boglund had said. "Holloway hasn't published anything, not even a book review. And his classroom performance is not acceptable either, as I've had to point out to him at every one of his performance reviews. He's conscientious, all right; weak students rate him quite high and comment on his willingness to help them. But even average students—let alone the good ones—flatly refuse to enroll in his sections of the introductory courses, and we'd never let him teach anything else. Those of his students who do go on to more advanced work find themselves hopelessly behind and usually drop out discouraged. Altogether in the final exams his students score twenty or more points below those in the other sections. If he belongs in teaching at all— and I've told him bluntly several times that he doesn't and should go back to industry and testing work—he belongs in high school."

So here were the Holloways to appeal against a decision they must know to be final and irrevocable. Under the university's bylaws, no different from those of any other respectable institution, the president could propose appointment after the probationary period only upon recommendation of the faculty in the field and of its chairman. Still he had no choice but to see them and to be as pleasant as he could.

To his surprise it was not the husband but the wife who spoke up. "Father President," she began, "a monstrous injustice is being done to my poor husband, whose only crime is that he is a true Christian in a university that calls itself Catholic but is dominated by heretics and Jews, and unbelievers. They deny reappointment to my husband, who goes to Mass every morning and works harder than any of them to help the weak students, and then they give tenure to three men whose names are Herzfeld, Abercrombie, and Yamanaka, and who have no time for undergraduates but remain closeted in their labs doing what they call research."

"You are unfair, Lisa," Holloway broke in; "those three men do good work."

"Oh, be quiet, Martin," she almost screamed, and two big red patches appeared on her cheeks. "He's just too simple, Father," she said, turning to Zimmerman, "and sees nothing but good in everybody, even when it's as obvious as the nose on my face what they're up to.

"You are a priest of Holy Church and President of this university. It's your sacred duty to stop these evildoers and their machinations. You'd expect such treachery in a secular university. But we chose St. Jerome when Martin got his doctorate precisely because we thought that in a Catholic university there's still some authority left, some decency and respect for religion and dedication."

"I am afraid," Heinz Zimmerman replied gently, "that you overrate both my power and my position. I am bound by the recommendation of the faculty. And I can assure you that the Regents, who make the final decision, would never appoint anyone who lacks faculty recommendation—even if I proposed him. You surely know that your husband's performance from the beginning did not satisfy our standards, whether in research or in teaching."

For a moment he thought she might attack him physically. Her face, which had been mottled before, turned a deep purple, her hands shook violently, and her eyes stared at him like those of a feral animal. He saw her husband cringe as if he himself expected a blow. But she controlled herself—barely, he thought—and hissed in a hoarse whisper:

"So you're in bed with them! Do you really think you can fool me with that pious cant about your power and your position? That the appraisals of Martin were negative only proves it. Your lot were out to get him from the beginning—the moment you discovered that we aren't apostates and hypocrites but take our religion seriously. You call this a Catholic university. But the girl students are shameless and sleep around openly, are painted like whores and smoke pot. And the faculty is worse. You have men who are divorced and have remarried, with their wives in the eyes of God still living. No wonder you can't abide God-fearing people like us and conspire to drive them out; we're a living reproof to you. You didn't dare refuse appointment to my husband three years ago—it would have been too obvious. But ever since, you, all of you, have plotted to get rid of him.

"But it won't be so easy—you haven't heard the last of it yet. I'll write to the bishop, and I'll write to the chairman of the Regents, and I'll write to the General of the Order—I'll do so today."

With that she yanked her husband out of the chair in which he had huddled in dejection, pushed him out of the room, and slammed the door.

A few seconds later Ritter came in with a wry half-smile on his face. "So, you too have joined the great anti-Catholic conspiracy of the priests of St. Jerome," he said.

"Of course," Heinz Zimmerman thought to himself when Erwin Ritter had again left his study, "the anti-Catholic conspiracy at St. Jerome is plain ludicrous. Four fifths of the faculty are Catholics except maybe in the Law School, and an

16

even larger proportion of the students—a percentage that won't change as far as I can see ahead. And then the wretched woman got her facts wrong. I can well believe that Herzfeld and Yamanaka aren't Catholics; but Abercrombie is, despite his Scots Calvinist name. He was an altar boy in high school and assists me regularly at Sunday Mass before we play tennis.

"But that's not really the point. In her demented, distorted harangue, that woman has raised a key question: What is a Catholic university and what should it be?

"I know the answer," Zimmerman went on to himself, "and have known it for more than twenty-five years. It's because I have known it that I became President of St. Jerome and have been able to transform this university from a parochial backwater with no more students than hundreds of other small denominational colleges, and a faculty not much different from what you'd find in a high school, into a national university with three or four potential Nobel Prizewinners on the faculty.

"But I also know that this Mrs. Holloway isn't the only one who refuses to accept the answer. Even Erwin Ritter doesn't, at least not wholeheartedly. And yet it was really my having the answer that made him push me all the way into the presidency of St. Jerome."

And Zimmerman's mind flashed back twenty-seven years to one of his first faculty meetings as a very young assistant professor, a few months after he had returned to St. Jerome from Germany, only recently ordained a priest and with a brand-new doctor's degree. Erwin Ritter had presided—he had just been appointed dean. As his first official act, he asked all faculty members to submit in writing their ideas for the future of St. Jerome. The university was then still quite small, only 2,400 students, all male, with a faculty of 120 or so, most of them priests. But Ritter had clearly foreseen the coming explosion of American higher education, "although even Erwin," thought Zimmerman, "could hardly have imagined that only twenty-five years later we would have more than twelve thousand students, two fifths of them women, and a faculty that will reach a thousand by next fall—all but a handful not priests but lay men and lay women."

A month or six weeks afterwards, at the next faculty meeting, Ritter had warmly thanked the faculty for its cooperation and praised the "many thoughtful memos I've received and will study carefully." But he had called in only one faculty member for further discussion: Heinz Zimmerman. "Heinz," he had said, "you wrote only two pages; most of the others wrote at least twenty. But your memo is the only one that says anything and really addresses St. Jerome's future.

"Yet what you say upsets me greatly, not because I disagree but because I have had to agree, despite misgivings and a great deal of internal resistance and discomfort."

And then Ritter, in that careful, precise, pedantic voice of his, had read out slowly the two-page memo Zimmerman had sent in:

November 15, 1952

Dear Father Dean:

For St. Jerome to survive, let alone to prosper, it must cease aiming at being a first-rate *Catholic* university and must instead aim at becoming a first-rate Catholic *university*.

Only a dozen years ago, before this country had entered World War II, to be a first-rate Catholic university in America meant being a first-rate Catholic institution and no worse than average as a center of teaching and learning, of scholarship and research, that is, as a university. When I first came to St. Jerome as a freshman just before Pearl Harbor, and when you, Dean Ritter, taught me in your first philosophy class as a newly appointed instructor and the youngest member of the faculty, Catholics, at least American-born ones, had to teach at a Catholic college or university; there were very few teaching jobs for them in other places. And even where Catholic students were being admitted freely, they were not exactly welcome.

All this, of course, had begun to change by the thirties, though slowly. But by now it's gone—only we refuse to accept it. Neither

Catholic scholars nor Catholic students any longer *have* to go to a Catholic school to teach or to learn. Indeed, more and more of the younger prominent Catholics have not attended Catholic schools but nondenominational ones; that rising political star, John F. Kennedy, who just got elected to the Senate from Massachusetts is but one example.

To be able to attract first-rate faculty and first-rate students, St. Jerome will therefore have to be a first-rate university first and a Catholic one second.

There is no alternative. To continue on the traditional course would condemn us—and fast—to becoming a game preserve for the third-rate among both Catholic scholars and Catholic students. Only if St. Jerome is accepted by the intellectual and scholarly communities in this country, and by American—and that means non-Catholic—public opinion, as one of the country's leading universities, will we of the Brotherhood of St. Jerome have remained true to the mission that our founder, Father Aloysius Schneider, the immigrant German priest, gave us almost exactly a century ago: "To be the spiritual and intellectual leaders of the Catholics in America."

"You frighten me, Heinz," Erwin Ritter had said, "and upset me. I've always regarded myself as a priest first and a scholar second. You demand me to change my whole life. But I have to admit that you're right."

From that day on, Erwin Ritter had been Zimmerman's sponsor, pushing him up the ladder step by step. Only four years later, Ritter had gotten Zimmerman promoted to assistant dean and moved into his own office. Two years after that, when Father Hasselmeier, the old president, became ill, Ritter had talked the Regents into naming Heinz Zimmerman assistant to the ailing man. Two more years and Father Hasselmeier had become so weak that he had to take a leave of absence. The Regents wanted to appoint Ritter acting president, but he turned them down, proposing Zimmerman instead. Another two years later, when Father Hasselmeier died, Ritter had declined once more and had again nominated Zimmerman for president of the university established by the

Confraternitas Sancti Hieronymi, the Brotherhood of St. Jerome, as a small college in 1892. "I know what needs to be done, but Heinz Zimmerman knows how to do it," he had said firmly.

Yet even Erwin Ritter was only persuaded and not truly convinced, to use the fine Socratic distinction he had tried so hard in his "Introductory Philosophy 101" to drill into eighteen-year-old Heinz Zimmerman, who until then had given little thought to anything except basketball and girls.

Only six weeks ago, recalled Zimmerman, Ritter at the annual meeting of the Catholic universities just after Christmas had come to him one evening and asked for a few minutes of his time.

"As you know," he began, "I'll be sixty-four by the end of this year and I've been dean for twenty-seven years, which is twenty years longer than anyone should hold the job. If the Good Lord gives me life and health, I'd like to stay on another six years—but not as dean. I'd like to go back into the classroom, that's where I was happiest. I intend to announce my resignation at Commencement in June to become effective at year end, on December 31. So you'd better spend a little time thinking through the specifications for my successor."

"That's easy," Zimmerman had responded immediately. "I'll delegate the assignment to the most qualified person, you."

"I thought you'd pull something like that," Erwin Ritter had said with his half-smile, "and I know the specs. The first two are not too hard to satisfy, especially if you move Sister Mary Annunciata of the Women's College into the job of budget director, which I'd recommend anyhow. First, you need someone the faculty and the deans of the schools can trust, accept, and respect. And secondly, the next dean of faculties needs to know how to balance educational and scholarly values and financial realities. It's the third qualification that bothers me.

"St. Jerome needs as its dean of faculties and its number

two executive under our structure—and the most likely candidate eventually to succeed you as chief executive—someone who believes in the first-rate Catholic university with both heart and head. You know that I fully accept it in my head, but I think you also know that I never quite got to fully believing it in my heart. That's not good enough for my successor. There are, of course, quite a few people at St. Jerome who believe in the first-rate university, without its necessarily being more than nominally Catholic—the very way perhaps that Princeton is still 'Calvinist.' And there are quite a few, if only among the older ones, who believe in the first-rate Catholic institution without its necessarily being any great shakes as a university. But I'm not sure there is anyone who believes with both head and heart in a St. Jerome that is first-rate both as a Catholic institution and as a university."

"I know Erwin is right," Heinz Zimmerman said to himself. "And I know that the St. Jerome faculty is not alone in its doubts. Anti-Catholics deny that it's possible at all. Three months ago I was raked over the coals in *The Voice of Reason* for my speech on 'The Great Catholic University in America,' and the writer trotted out all the old clichés, the Inquisition, the Index of Forbidden Books, the doctrine of papal infallibility, to argue that a Catholic university is a contradiction in terms. But even our own bishop here in Capital City feels much the same way, I have a hunch. Last year at Commencement when he spent an hour resting in my office, he spotted the trophy wall and saw that I'd put my honorary doctorate from Columbia up at the top rather than the one from Notre Dame. He shook his head and said, 'Does this mean, Heinz, that being a great university requires being secular, if not Godless and atheist?'

"But I know I'm right. And if it doesn't work, there won't be a St. Jerome twenty years hence. If it doesn't work there won't be intellectual excellence and leadership in this country at all except from what the bishop calls the Godless and the atheists. And I know it can work. I know it isn't true that a first-rate scientist can't be both a Christian and a Catholic. And I also know it isn't true, as that dreadful woman, Mrs. Holloway, wants us to believe, that being a good Catholic excuses being an incompetent scientist.

"Then why did the Holloways upset me so much?

"It's not the Holloway *woman* who upsets me," he suddenly realized. "It's the husband." The moment he said it to himself, he knew it to be true. At once he saw again in his mind's eye that tall scarecrow of a man huddling in despair in the chair, his face buried in his hands, ashamed to the very core of his being, of himself and even more of that harridan, frightened of her but completely dominated by her—defeated by life, by his sense of incompetence, and by the open contempt of his own wife.

"What really upsets me," Heinz Zimmerman said out loud, aimlessly swishing the spoon around in the cup of coffee Agnes had brought in twenty minutes earlier but from which he had not yet drunk, "is my own attitude toward Martin Holloway. I feel guilty. Not because I can't renew his contract or change the poor devil's marriage. I feel guilty because I have not one shred of pity or compassion for him, his suffering or his degradation. All I feel is infinite contempt.

"No human being should have to look the way he did yesterday. And instead of feeling sorry for him, I despised him, hated him for his incompetence, his abject failure, his weakness and cowardice. *She* only bothered me; but he offended, humiliated, and hurt me."

That despicable woman had invoked his "sacred duty" as president of the university and as a priest. Well, he had a duty as president, sacred or profane, to prevent Holloway's continuing at St. Jerome. But didn't he also have some kind of duty as a priest, or perhaps even only as a Christian? A duty to relieve that poor creature, Martin Holloway's, self-loathing— the self-loathing from which he had shrunk as from the stench of an oozing plague boil. "It is my bounden duty," Heinz Zimmerman, Christian and priest, said to himself, almost as

22

in prayer, "to succor the sick and to wash and bind up the wounds of the flesh. Isn't it my duty as well to wash and bind up the wounds of the spirit?

"I know that it's not a matter of money or of a job. Clem told me that Holloway can easily get back the kind of job in industry he had before he left to get his Ph. D. And in industry he'll make far more than what we can pay an assistant professor."

Holloway must know this, if only, thought Zimmerman, because Boglund, who looked after his Chemistry faculty like a mother hen, had surely told him. "It must be his failure as an academic, as a teacher and scholar, rather than any material threat that has destroyed his self-respect and earned him the scathing contempt of his wife. And yet, if Holloway can be a teacher at all, Boglund said, it could only be at the high-school level.

"But where just recently have I heard someone talk of needing conscientious high-school-level science teachers in college jobs? I know. It was Louise McCollough."

At once Zimmerman saw before him the tall, raw-boned Mrs. McCollough, only recently arrived from a deanship at Smith, or Wellesley, or some such Eastern women's school to assume the presidency of Harriet Beecher Stowe, the women's college on the other, northern side of Capital City. She was sitting bolt upright in the chair across from him with her New England boarding school posture and saying in her clear New England boarding school voice:

"Your agreeing to let our upper-class women who need advanced work in the sciences attend classes and get grades at St. Jerome is more of a help to us than you can realize, Father Zimmerman. It solves half of my problem—the easier half, I'm afraid."

"And what is the tougher half?" Zimmerman had asked.

"Oh, you know the answer, Father," Mrs. McCollough responded with a shrug of her shoulders. "It's the perennial problem of a women's college: how to attract and hold science faculty who have the credentials for college teaching and then have to do what is really high-school work, year in and year out, and do so conscientiously.

"The introductory-level courses in the sciences for the first- and second-year students we cannot subcontract but have to provide ourselves, if only because the numbers are so large: between six and seven hundred as against the sixty or seventy each year who intend to major in a science or go to medical school and need advanced work. And the instructors must have a Ph.D. and must have taught for a few years in a major university, or else we risk losing accreditation and not getting our graduates into medical or graduate schools. Yet no one with those kind of qualifications is likely to be willing to teach kids who mostly have no science background and no science interest, and are only taking the courses because we require two semesters of science for the degree . . . and fully intend, I can assure you, to continue to do so.

"No, pay isn't the problem. We are able to pay quite well. But qualified people consider this work demeaning. 'If I had wanted to teach high school, I wouldn't have spent six years of my life getting my Ph.D. in physics,' my best young science teacher said to me a few weeks ago when she came in to tell me that she's taking a job as a researcher at Bell Lab. And I am afraid I'd have to agree with her."

Louise McCollough wasn't the type of woman Zimmerman particularly liked; not enough of a sense of humor and too much of a sense of superiority, he thought. But she had a mind he respected—cool, crisp, facing realities, and not afraid of saying or doing unconventional things like contracting out her advanced science courses.

And so now, without further thought, he took the phone, dialed her number, and said to her:

"Remember our talk in my office just before Christmas about your difficulty in getting qualified people to teach the introductory science courses at Harriet Beecher Stowe? Maybe I can help a little. I may have a man who has the qualifications to satisfy accrediting boards and medical school deans and yet is willing to teach chemistry at the high-school level to students without much background, and to do so conscientiously."

When he had hung up, he felt at first greatly relieved. "I really should call in Agnes and tell her," he thought, almost getting out of his chair to open the door and speak to her. Then he hesitated. Agnes would not approve. Indeed, he knew that she'd call him "Father President," as she only did when she was strongly opposed to something he wanted to do.

"Father President," she'd say, "you are always so wonderfully kind and considerate, but in this case your kindness strikes me as somewhat unwarranted. Should the President of St. Jerome really go job-hunting for an incompetent assistant professor? And can you truly recommend this Professor Holloway in light of what Dean Ritter and Professor Boglund have told you about him? May I suggest"—Agnes was strong on suggesting—"that you tell Professor Boglund of the possible interest at Harriet Beecher Stowe and then leave it to him to advise Professor Holloway to apply there, provided of course he feels he can support Holloway?"

Was Agnes right? Had he acted rashly and let his heart overrule his head? Or had he simply acted in self-indulgence to make himself feel better? Or—and the thought made Heinz Zimmerman blanch—had he in fact been intimidated by that dreadful woman, the wife, and acted to appease that she-devil rather than out of any Christian duty to help the poor husband?

The more Heinz Zimmerman thought about his phone call to Louise McCollough, the less sure he became that it had been the right thing to do. "It's trivial," he thought, "but it bothers me. I need to tell someone, someone I know and trust, if only to be told 'Don't worry.'

"I can't tell Agnes, and I rather think I don't want to discuss it with Erwin. He dislikes my concerning myself with faculty matters he thinks are his concern; he'd call it meddling. What about Seymour Bercovitz?"

Unlike Erwin Ritter, whom he had known for forty years, and Agnes Muller, whom he had known for twenty, Seymour Bercovitz, M.D., Professor of Psychiatry, chairman of the Department of Community Medicine at the state university's Medical School, and State Commissioner of Mental Health, had only recently become Heinz Zimmerman's friend.

They had met six years earlier when serving together on a State Commission on Mental Health. From the first they had found each other *simpatico*. Eventually they wrote the Commission's report together, which led to the appointment of a State Commissioner of Mental Health as a member of the governor's cabinet. They had, Heinz Zimmerman felt, very much the same kind of mind and the same sense of humor. And he enjoyed the salty Jewish stories Berkovitz told with tongue-in-cheek seriousness in a rasping Brooklyn accent. But there was also something faintly clerical about the short yet dignified doctor, with his carefully trimmed, slightly graying beard and his controlled, precise gestures—"very much like those of a priest saying Mass," Zimmerman had once thought. He was not surprised when he learned later that Bercovitz's father had been a rabbi and that Bercovitz himself had started out to study for the rabbinate before switching to medicine.

Over the years Heinz Zimmerman and Dr. Bercovitz had come to see more and more of each other. Both were enthusiastic though thoroughly mediocre chess players, and their chess evening had become a weekly event, with Bercovitz cooking a simple but exquisite meal and Zimmerman providing a bottle of wine. But it had taken a long time before Bercovitz began to talk about himself, though he was intensely lonely and needed a friend. About five years younger than Zimmerman, he had been a widower for almost a decade. His wife, whom he had loved deeply, had been killed in

26

an automobile accident shortly after he moved to Capital City as Professor of Psychiatry from his native New York, and had left him alone with two children, a boy and a girl, both now teenagers. He was totally wrapped up in them: "They are my trust from Lillian," he had once said in a rare outburst of confidence. "I know I need to remarry, and there'd be no lack of candidates; but Lillian's children would feel betrayed."

Gradually Berkovitz had also begun to talk about other problems, and especially the ones he faced in so political a job as State Commissioner of Mental Health—first to Heinz Zimmerman, and then increasingly also to Agnes Muller, who had come to approve highly of the quiet, reserved man with his courtly, almost Old World manners.

But Bercovitz had only become a real friend a few months ago when he had said "No" to Heinz Zimmerman. For several years Zimmerman had planned to enlarge his board and include a few prominent non-Catholics. "After all," he had said to Bercovitz, "St. Jerome is the leading private and non-governmental institution of higher learning in the state." He knew that his Regents would not swallow a Protestant yet, but what about a prominent Jew? And if a Jew, who better qualified than a leading physician, chairman of a department in the Medical School, and a high state official? Yet when he broached the idea to Bercovitz, he met with a flat refusal.

"I am touched and honored, Father Heinz," Bercovitz had said. "And I am greatly tempted. But you'd damage the university, and I can't let you do that. You'd only offend the prominent Jews in Capital City, the very people whose support and money you need.

"You don't understand? Then I'm afraid I have to bore you with a piece of personal history. I told you, didn't I, that I started out to become a rabbi like my father? But I dropped out of the seminary in my second year. It was in the late forties and Israel had just become an independent state. And I don't think, Father Heinz, you can imagine what that meant to us American Jews. Every one of us suddenly felt three feet taller.

"Have you ever heard of an Englishman named Victor Gollancz? No reason why you should, of course. He was an English publisher, a very well-known and successful one, a prominent figure in world Jewry and an ardent Zionist from way back. But when the Israelis drove out the Arabs, Gollancz broke with them. The Jews, he wrote in books and articles and pamphlets, had just suffered the worst persecution of any people in history for no other crime than that of being Jews. And immediately upon getting themselves a little power, they persecuted the Arabs and drove them out of lands they had peacefully farmed for more than a thousand years, making them homeless for no other crime than their not being Jews.

"Gollancz was considered a traitor by Jews everywhere, and especially, of course, by Zionists—and I was an ardent one. But he shook me profoundly. I prayed and I prayed but I got no answer. What almost destroyed me was not that I had to agree with Gollancz. It was that I saw no alternative for the Israeli. What the Jews did to the Palestinians, I had to agree with Gollancz, was a sin and not too different from what Hitler had done to the Jews. But what alternative did the Israelis have? What way out was there other than to heap persecution upon persecution, injustice upon injustice, sin upon sin?

"And then I lost my faith in God. It had been hard enough for a Jew, believe me, to accept His allowing the fate that had been meted out to us in the Holocaust. But if even God could not find any other solution for saving the Children of Israel than for them to become like their persecutors, then where was His wisdom, His mercy, His power? He was no better than any of us; indeed, there was no God in whom I could have faith. What could I have said to my congregation about this God? How could I have promised them that God would reward virtue and righteousness and punish vice? How could I have solaced the afflicted?

"And so," Seymour Bercovitz continued, "I decided to give up becoming a minister to the afflicted and a healer of souls and switched instead to healing the sicknesses of the mind.

"But this also means that I am not much of a Zionist anymore. Of course I haven't told anyone this story. You're only the third person after my father, who was greatly hurt when I dropped out of the seminary, and my wife. But where other Jews are concerned, Jews have good noses. The Jews in Capital City whose support and money you need at St. Jerome, the Kesslers and the Fynemans and Judge Rosenbaum, all know that I don't buy State of Israel bonds or appear when the Israeli ambassador comes to town. They don't say it to my face; but in their eyes, I am a kind of traitor. So I could only harm you if I joined your board."

"But can't I bring you in at all?" Zimmerman had pleaded.

"You can always count on me as a member of your kitchen cabinet," Bercovitz had said with a smile and a firm handshake. And from that moment Zimmerman had considered Bercovitz a friend. So why not talk to him about that Holloway business? He could almost hear Bercovitz saying as he had said so many times in the past, "It's nothing, Father Heinz. Just a small pebble in the shoe."

But when he reached Bercovitz on the telephone at his office, the doctor, after listening for a few moments, said with quite unusual sharpness: "Go back to the beginning and tell me everything, every little detail, every word you can remember. When and how did you first come into contact with these people? Begin there, and leave nothing out."

After the whole story had been told, there was such a long silence at the other end that Heinz Zimmerman asked twice: "Seymour, are you still there?" until Bercovitz finally spoke.

"In all likelihood this is the end of the affair and there is nothing to worry about. But, Heinz"—and Zimmerman realized with a start that Bercovitz had called him Heinz for the first time instead of Father Heinz—"you shouldn't have made that phone call to Harriet Beecher Stowe. We all do it, of course, it's almost impossible to resist the temptation to appease a paranoid. And I've no business making such a diagnosis without even having seen the woman. But the fact that they create guilt feelings in normal people is the hallmark of paranoids and what makes them so dangerous. Appeasement only confirms them in their delusion, that's the very nature of their sickness. Well, in all probability it's only a small pebble in the shoe. But I still wish you hadn't made that phone call."

And when he hung up, Bercovitz murmured to himself, "A nasty business. I don't like it at all."

PART TWO

"**A**re there any more letters or reports, Tom?" asked Bishop O'Malley.

"One more, Bishop," Father Martini, the bishop's secretary, replied. "It was delivered by hand last night, in a St. Jerome University envelope marked 'Personal.' I don't think I should open it."

The bishop tore open the envelope and extracted six handwritten sheets. He took one look at the signature, muttered, "I don't think I know this person or have ever heard of her," and handed the letter back to Tom. "Read it and tell me what's it all about."

"It's from a Mrs. Lisa Holloway," Martini began, after quickly scanning the six pages. "Her husband, his first name is Martin, is an assistant professor of chemistry at St. Jerome University, has been there three years. He is apparently an older man.

"'When I first met him,' she writes, 'he lived a life without God and served Mammon. With the help of the Holy Spirit I was able to lead him into the True Catholic Church and to make him dedicate himself to educating the young.'"

The bishop made a sound—whether chuckle or groan was hard to tell. But when Martini looked up, he only said, "Go on, Tom."

"'And now, the Chemistry faculty and the department chairman have unanimously recommended that his contract not be renewed. And Father Zimmerman, the President, refuses to intervene.'"

"Of course," said the bishop.

"But," continued Martini, "she writes that her husband's only fault—I am quoting, sir—is that they are good Catholics and he is the victim of a rampant anti-Catholic conspiracy at St. Jerome University. 'It isn't only,' she writes, 'that my husband is being fired when three men who are much younger, Herzfeld, Abercrombie, and Yamanaka—hardly good Catholic names—are being reappointed to tenure-track positions. A few months ago, to the great shock and pain of all good Catholics on the St. Jerome faculty, the associate dean of the Law School, Father Breuner'" ("That old windbag," interjected the bishop), "'a distinguished canonist, an experienced administrator, and a pillar of the true faith, was pointedly passed over, and a Jewish tax lawyer who is only interested in saving the rich money was appointed Law School dean.'

"And then," said Martini, "she goes on to say that the university is being given over to domination by heretics and unbelievers and Jews with the full connivance of its President, and that the students who come to St. Jerome because their parents expect them to be nurtured there in Christian values and the Catholic tradition are instead led into lives of vice, debauchery, and Godlessness—and so on and so on."

"You know what to do, I'm sure," said the bishop.

"Yes, sir. I'll send her a note telling her that the university and the Brotherhood of St. Jerome are autonomous and not under your control."

"Right. And send Father Zimmerman a Xerox copy of the woman's letter and a copy of your note to her, with my compliments."

"Is that necessary?" asked Martini.

"Of course. Why do you ask?"

"There is one paragraph in the letter, Bishop," said Martini, blushing a little, "that might offend Father Zimmerman."

"Read it to me," said the bishop, "and don't pussyfoot."

"'And in a university that calls itself Catholic,'" Martini read out, "'and is supposed to set an example of Christian virtue and moral living, the President, an ordained priest of Holy Church, gives grave offense by sharing an office with a woman much younger than he, who is constantly in his company and who openly without even attempting discretion visits him at the President's residence most Sundays under the pretext of taking work to him. Much as it pains me, I have to submit to Your Excellency that such conduct on the part of an ordained priest calls for a most shameful interpretation.' Bitch," added Tom Martini, half under his breath.

"Now, Father, that's no language for a priest to use." But while the words were a formal reprimand, there was no reproach in the bishop's voice, and he immediately added: "A vile woman, all right, and a slanderer to boot. I don't think you know Father Zimmerman well, Tom, do you? Believe me, there's no better priest in the diocese, whatever one might think of some of his educational ideas. And the lady in question is about as decent a woman as you could hope to find anywhere, and a crackerjack at her job. Have you met Agnes Muller, Father Zimmerman's assistant at St. Jerome? If Canon Law allowed putting a lay person, let alone a woman, in the position, I'd have tried long ago to lure her away from St. Jerome and put her in here as Vicar General—I don't know an abler executive.

"To be sure," the bishop went on, "this piece of garbage makes it all the more necessary to send the letter and a copy of your note to Father Zimmerman. But I'd better add a personal word to him.

"Write: 'Dear Heinz: We all get letters like this once in a while and have learned to disregard them. But should you decide to take disciplinary action against the writer, I'd understand it and would support you.

"'Yours Faithfully in Christ,' and bring it to me for my signature.

"And now, Tom, I want you to go to Monsignor Murtagh's office. I asked him two weeks ago to get me the figures and projections for total population and Catholic population for the state and each county in it, and he phoned me Friday afternoon that they're ready. Go over the figures with Bernie Murtagh till you're absolutely sure they are correct; you know Bernie can be a little slipshod. And I want you to know those figures by heart, forward and backward.

"Why, you ask? I'll tell you—but please don't tell anyone else, least of all Murtagh.

"I've decided to appoint a Senior Vice Chancellor or a Deputy Vicar General—I'll let Rome worry about the title—as my deputy and representative in Palmer, and have the Western counties work directly with him. No other state of the Union has a Catholic population growing at a faster rate; and the forecast is for even speedier growth, especially in the West, with the steady influx of immigrants from Mexico. The diocese already has a larger Catholic population than any other in the country except Brooklyn—and that's a special case, right next to the New York Archdiocese and really part of it. It violates every principle of organization to centralize everything here in Capital City. That's why all the vice chancellors are bogged down in paperwork and no one can get a decision out of this office.

"But I don't have to tell you," the bishop continued, "that what I propose is against tradition and convention, though there is nothing in Canon Law that forbids it, and a few precedents. I'll have to make out a strong case with the Nuncio when I see him in Washington on Friday. I don't expect any major problems. Allessandri, the Nuncio's counselor, is all for it. Still, you'd better have the figures at your fingertips and know how to present them if there are questions."

"Whom would you put into Palmer?" Martini asked.

"Whom would *you* put in, Tom?" was the bishop's rejoinder.

"Probably Monsignor Sullivan," Martini said, after a moment's thought. "He's the senior vice chancellor and he is sixty-six."

The bishop laughed with pleasure. "Right on the button,

Tom. Of course I plan to appoint Sullivan. His age will ensure that he and everybody else knows it's his terminal job. He'll reach retirement age before I do, being three years older. By then Rome will have had enough time to pick their own man."

"And," said Martini, "to pick the first Bishop of Palmer."

"Precisely," said the bishop, "and high time too. I plan— but please, Tom, this is for your ears only—to ask the Nuncio that he recommend to Rome that Palmer be made a diocese (it has more than enough Catholics already) and that Capital City be raised to an archdiocese. I strongly suspect that Rome intended to do this fifteen years ago when my predecessor died. But he left behind such a financial mess that the plan had to be shelved. Mind you, Tom, Bishop Byrne was a wonderful man, a first-rate theologian and a fine teacher. I owe him a lot—he was rector of the Diocesan Seminary when I was a student there and couldn't have been kinder or more generous to me. But he was no administrator and the diocese was on the brink of financial disaster. That's when the Nuncio called me in—an auxiliary bishop in northern California— and said, 'You'll be the first diocesan ever chosen by the Holy Father because he has an MBA degree.' But you've heard all this before."

Tom nodded, with a smile.

"You know, Tom," the bishop went on, "that I'm far from satisfied with the financial condition of the diocese. It's still quite precarious. But at least we aren't bankrupt and we're in better shape than most of the other dioceses in North America. And now I think I can revive the archdiocesan idea. Of course, Rome likes to do such things when there is a change anyhow. But if my successor is to be consecrated Archbishop of Capital City, we'd better start now. The longest I have is twelve years and Rome likes to take its time. And I *do* want to have been the last bishop of Capital City, so make sure of those figures and projections."

As Tom Martini was about to leave the room, the bishop added:

"Come back in an hour, please. That should give me time to go over these budget figures of yours on our hospitals. And make an appointment with Monsignor Duffy to discuss the budgets either tomorrow afternoon or Wednesday first thing in the morning. I want to run through the hospital budgets before you and I leave for Washington on Wednesday afternoon."

Then the bishop reached across and picked up a blue folder marked "Hospitals—1980/81" that had been lying on Father Martini's side of the desk. But instead of reading it, he leaned back in his chair and murmured to himself: "I wonder whether even Tom guesses the most important item on the Washington agenda: Thomas Martini himself, and his future."

Bishop O'Malley never kept a secretary for more than four years. He was convinced that staying on longer in the job did permanent damage to a young priest. Either he'd become a "subordinate" and thus forever remain a clerk, unable to make a decision of his own; or, worse, he'd become a wire-puller who abused the close personal relationship to the "boss" to lord it over the diocesan clergy. And Tom Martini had been O'Malley's secretary—his fourth since he had come to Capital City as its bishop fifteen years ago—for a little over three and a half years now.

"Of course," said Patrick O'Malley to himself, "I could do with Tom what I did with his predecessors, make him a vice chancellor. But it's not the right job for Tom. He needs greater exposure than the little world of Capital City—and he needs to be known in a greater world, too. What he really needs is the kind of experience I was lucky to have at his age, as an associate secretary, say, at the National Conference of Catholic Bishops in Washington, or an attaché in the Nuncio's office."

Tom Martini had not been O'Malley's first choice when Father Duffy had neared the end of his four years as the bishop's secretary. O'Malley did not even think of choosing any but an Irishman for the job—someone like himself and his three earlier secretaries, who had grown up in the same Irish-American working-class world, with a staunch trade unionist for a father, someone who spoke the same language and looked the same.

But a few weeks before Father Duffy was to move out, O'Malley had been invited to Washington together with a handful of fellow bishops as dinner guests of the newly arrived counselor to the Nuncio, Monsignor Allessandri. And Allessandri had said in that near-perfect "English" English he had acquired at Oxford, and in the half-joking tone he always affected when he wanted to say something especially serious: "In the few months I've been in the United States, I've learned what extraordinary people you Irish-Americans are"—his guests, all being Irish, chuckled. "But the Irish, I take it, are a small minority among American Catholics, and a small minority even among American Catholic priests. Yet every one of your secretaries I've met today for the first time, and an impressive group they are, has an Irish name. Are there no young able priests around who aren't Irish?"

The others had laughed it off. But O'Malley was thunderstruck. If there was one thing he believed in, one thing he'd learned in the evening classes in management he'd attended at George Washington after obtaining his doctorate in Canon Law at Georgetown, one thing he then taught in his own classes in management and organization as a young adjunct professor, it was that an executive must consider *all* the people in his organization for training, development, and promotion. And yet in his own practice he had totally disregarded this elementary rule.

There was an explanation, of course. In his formative years, from the time when, as a very young priest, he had been sent to Washington a few months after Pearl Harbor to help organize the Chaplain Corps for the armed services until, twenty years later, he was appointed auxiliary bishop to a near-bankrupt diocese in northern California and given the job of straightening out its finances, he had worked directly under

Cardinal Spellman of New York, had been taught by him, formed by him, and had come to admire Spellman profoundly. And for Spellman, despite (or perhaps, because of) all his years in Rome before becoming Cardinal-Archbishop of New York, the Catholic Church in America was an Irish Church and ordained to remain an Irish Church.

But that was clearly no excuse. And so, as soon as he returned from that trip to Washington, O'Malley began to look for a non-Irish successor to Gerald Duffy.

Tom Martini emerged almost immediately as the leading candidate. He was the right age, thirty-one, and had been a priest for five years. He had graduated at the top of his class in the joint five-year college-seminary program which Bishop O'Malley had worked out with Father Heinz Zimmerman of St. Jerome University for the diocesan seminarians. He had then spent four years at the Gregorian University in Rome, earning a doctorate with honors in medieval history and medieval philosophy, and steeping himself in Dante. Then, after returning to his native Capital City, he had become an assistant pastor at St. Anne's, where he handled administration and finance for the diocese's largest parish.

From his first day as the bishop's secretary, Martini had performed better than any of his predecessors, sure-footed, with tact, exquisite courtesy, and just the right mixture of deference and independence. Above all, from the first day he had displayed great ability with both people and numbers.

"Tom Martini," the bishop had once told Allessandri, "is better with numbers than I am, despite my MBA in finance and accounting. Yet people don't think him cold and don't resent him. I know that I'm not loved by my clergy and the young priests call me 'His Efficiency' instead of 'His Excellency' behind my back. Martini is far more budget-conscious than I am. But they like him even when he kills off their pet projects and cuts their appropriations by seventy percent."

And yet O'Malley was at first not at all comfortable with his new secretary. He used to ask himself whether he'd have felt the same if the name had been Martin instead of Martini; but, no, it went much deeper than that. The young priest was just too different from anything an O'Malley was used to.

"All his four grandparents," the bishop said to himself, "were dirt-poor like mine, and like the grandparents of all the rest of us; landless farm laborers as far back as anyone could trace their ancestry. It shouldn't really make a difference that his came from Calabria and Apulia and mine from County Mayo—peasants are peasants everywhere. I'll never look like anything else, nor will Murtagh or Duffy or Corrigan, no matter how many doctorates or titles we earn. All right, I'm the gaunt peasant with the pot belly, and Murtagh is the roly-poly one, but no one will ever mistake either of us for anything but the shanty Irish we are.

"But this young priest, this Italian peasant boy, looks to the purple born—he really looks like a Prince of the Church. And he walks and talks and sits like one, and wears his well-worn clothes like a cardinal's robes. He's like a figure in an early Italian painting, a Duccio perhaps, or one of the other early Sienese, a youthful St. John the Baptist or a St. Sebastian in his martyrdom, with that radiant smile and manly beauty but also with a saint's ascetism and other-worldliness."

O'Malley had felt so uncomfortable with his new secretary that he thought it his duty to mention it to the young man and to apologize for his parochial prejudices. Tom Martini had laughed good-humoredly and said: "I hope you'll not think me presumptuous, sir, if I say that I know exactly how you must feel with a Martini instead of a Martin. It's how we Martinis and Calabreses and Antonellis and all of us in Little Italy felt when we heard that a Pole had been elected Pope. My grand-father was still alive then—his name was Buonsegni—and he said, 'Thank God, it could have been worse; it could have been an Irish.'" They had both roared with laughter. And from then on there was no more uneasiness.

"Tom is an extraordinary person"—thought O'Malley—"a far abler man than I am or ever could have been, a far abler man than a good many of my colleagues among the American bishops." And now the time had come to think of Tom's next assignment, which would be crucial to his career.

The door opened and Martini was back.

"Here are the population figures, all checked out," he said; "and the letter to Father Zimmerman for you to sign. And I've arranged for the conference on the hospital budgets to be held in this office at three tomorrow afternoon."

"Good work, Tom," said the bishop, as he signed the Zimmerman letter. "And now we really must go to work on those hospital budgets—I need you to tell me where all the corpses are buried."

But instead, O'Malley found himself talking again of St. Jerome University and of Heinz Zimmerman.

"I respect Father Zimmerman, and admire his achievements at St. Jerome. I have absolute trust in his integrity as a man and as a priest. But I fear he's headed for real trouble. I don't think his 'Great Catholic University' can possibly work. And he's so completely wrapped up in it that even a slight setback might shatter him."

"I don't follow you, sir," said Martini. "Every book or magazine article about American higher education, whether by a Catholic or a non-Catholic, holds up St. Jerome as the very model of success."

"But that's the surface," said the bishop. "Enrollment and endowment and the number of prizes and awards the faculty gets. But the core is hollow.

"Tell me, Tom, have you read Father Zimmerman's paper on the Catholic University in America?"

"Of course, sir, you distributed it to all the clergy in the diocese."

"It's a brilliant piece of work. It gave me an entirely new perspective, but not, I'm afraid, the one Zimmerman wanted his readers to get. It explained to me for the first time why we have Catholic colleges and Catholic universities in this country. All of us in the American Catholic Church always thought that we have them to teach Catholic students Catholic values—I bet you think so, too?"

Martini nodded.

"But Zimmerman proves that that was not the real reason. We have Catholic colleges and universities in America because the United States has been so Protestant and anti-Catholic that otherwise Catholics would have had no access to secular learning. Catholic teachers would have been denied jobs in non-Catholic universities and Catholic students would have had a hard time getting admitted. We needed our own schools, not to preserve Catholic values, but to acquire the secular skills of a modern society. Zimmerman didn't say it— and I doubt whether he even sees it. But the way he presents it, the Catholic college in America isn't that much different from the Negro colleges in the South which came into being because black teachers and black students couldn't otherwise gain access to the learning and the skills of the white society around them.

"Father Zimmerman," the bishop continued, "likes to quote that great Franciscan saint and philosopher St. Bonaventure, who, as you once told me, Tom, influenced Dante so greatly, and who wrote that lovely little pamphlet *How All Knowledge Leads Back to the Knowledge of God*. It's true enough, of course, for a Christian, but it's not true in the way Zimmerman interprets it. In the twentieth century, knowledge has become thoroughly secular and leads nowhere except to more secular knowledge."

"Yes," commented Martini, "if the dean of the St. Jerome Law School were a Catholic priest and indeed a 'pillar of the true faith,' to quote that horrible woman's letter, tax law would still not lead anywhere near the Knowledge of God."

"Nor," said the bishop dryly, "would the course in Chemical Analysis, even if taught by the most devoutly Catholic Professor Holloway.

"You know, Tom, after I'd read Zimmerman's paper I sent to the library for the catalogues of all the St. Jerome colleges and schools—quite a collection, running to several thousand pages of course offerings. And I couldn't find more than a mere handful of courses that might have anything to do with the Knowledge of God or leading a student there. In fact, I could find very little difference between what St. Jerome and the most un-Catholic university would offer."

"But, Bishop," protested Martini, "in that case why do you stress learning as much as you do and demand that all priests in the diocese get an advanced degree in some academic or professional discipline?"

"A priest is a generalist, Tom, and generalists need to have one area in which they are experts and can be held to standards of craftsmanship. Otherwise they become dilettantes. That's a sound principle of management. But also the priest is no longer the only literate person in an illiterate society. He has to be equal in learning and skill to the educated laity in order to command their respect, and should really be their superior." ("Here he goes again," thought Martini to himself with a groan. "Whenever I'm in here, I feel like a character in a platonic dialogue. All they do is say every five pages, 'It would indeed seem so, Socrates.' Well, they learned—and I certainly do.")

The bishop meanwhile had been silent for a minute, but now he began again.

"Zimmerman is quite right. The discrimination against Catholics as teachers and students on the part of non-Catholic institutions is gone, or going fast. And then the traditional Catholic university cannot survive in America if it stays second-rate. But if his premise is correct—and he has completely convinced me—and the purpose of the Catholic universities in this country was to give Catholics access to secular learning, then his conclusion is a logical fallacy. In fact, I'm surprised that he didn't see this—after all, he was a Professor of Logic and, so I'm told, a good one. From his premise there follows only one conclusion, and an inescapable one, I'd say. The more a university succeeds in becoming a 'great university,' the more completely secular it must become. It cannot be both a 'great university' and a 'Catholic university.' The only logical conclusion from Father Zimmerman's premise is to do what the Protestants, Harvard and Yale and Princeton and Columbia, did a hundred years ago: becoming nonsectarian and nondenominational and cut all ties to organized religion. It hasn't done them any harm; but it also didn't do the Protestant denominations any harm, as far as I can judge.

"I know my fellow bishops think this heresy, and I haven't even dared mention it to Heinz Zimmerman. But do you see any other conclusion that makes logical sense?"

"Isn't there," Martini asked, "another possible conclusion: to go 'fundamentalist,' as so many of the small Protestant colleges have been doing quite successfully?"

"In theory, yes," said the bishop, "but only in theory. In practice it's seven hundred years too late. That was, of course, what the fundamentalists of the thirteenth century wanted, those anti-intellectual Franciscan *Illuminati* against whom St. Bonaventure wrote his little book. You know, Tom, of all the philosophy I had to read in the seminary I enjoyed that pamphlet the most, though otherwise I didn't ever understand one sentence St. Bonaventure wrote. Maybe fundamentalism would have worked at that point. But since then there has been too much scholarship and learning in the Church, and too much humanism and painting and music. A Catholic, I realize, should not be a rationalist, as so much of modern learning is. But he can even less afford to be anti-intellectual, as fundamentalists have to be. Whenever we try, we immediately come to look like those horrible, eroded, intellectually bankrupt small schools I have to visit and make polite noises about—St. Joseph's in Palmer, for instance, or St. Roche in Buffalo Junction where I was born—self-styled 'colleges' which are really just second-rate kindergartens with a football team and fraudulent pretensions. They always seem to me to be outrageous caricatures of those obscurantist Jesuit schools in Dublin that James Joyce described in *Portrait of the Artist as a Young Man*. Maybe they can survive in Ireland—it's amazing how many things can survive there. But Zimmerman is right, in our competitive climate here they're doomed."

"This bishop of mine," Tom Martini said to himself with an inward smile, "is as full of goodies as a plum pudding. My friends call him 'His Efficiency' and wince when he talks of management principles and cost/efficiency ratios—the very things we went into the Church to get away from. And he's amazingly good at it. I've learned more about management and organization, finance and marketing, from him than I would have learned at the Harvard Business School where my dad hoped I'd go. Then he talks about St. Bonaventure and alludes to an obscure episode in Church history. And now he's trotting out *Portrait of the Artist as a Young Man,* which I always thought a good Irish Catholic wasn't supposed to have heard of, let alone to have read."

The bishop was still pursuing the same train of thought. "In Roman Law there is a proverb: 'What is flawed from the beginning can never be made whole.' That, I am quite sure, applies to Father Zimmerman's university. Okay, St. Jerome may be able to retain a few outward vestiges of a religious past—no unisex dorms, for instance, and no free abortions for women students."

"But if those things become general in the outside world, Bishop," said Martini, "then I'd say even St. Jerome would have to accept them in the end."

"I don't intend to be around that long, Tom," the bishop said. "But you're right. Sooner or later—and I'd say sooner— Zimmerman's very success will force St. Jerome into choosing between being a 'great university,' as he phrases it, on a par with the leaders, or remaining a Catholic institution in any sense whatever. I don't think Zimmerman can face up to this decision—I'm very much afraid it would destroy him. But I do respect him, Tom, and think him the finest priest in my diocese."

"He isn't particularly popular, sir," said Martini. "I've heard him called vain and stuck-up more than once."

The bishop chuckled. "Oh, yes, the famous trophy wall. But believe me, Tom, that's no more serious than a ten-year-old girl putting a ribbon in her hair and admiring herself in the mirror.

"No, Heinz Zimmerman's real problem is a great deal more serious than a little childish vanity. He's one of those who don't know that they are intensely ambitious."

"I don't think I understand, Bishop."

"'Blessed are the Meek,' it says in the Beatitudes. But you know, Tom, I've never seen the meek make a contribution or achieve anything. The achievers are all people who think enough of themselves to make high demands on themselves, people who are highly ambitious. It's a theological riddle I've long ago given up on.

"But some of them, and often the highest achievers, don't realize that they are ambitious—and Heinz Zimmerman is one such. He is convinced, I'm sure, that in all he does he is motivated solely by his desire to serve his Order, his university, and the Church. The rest of us know very well that our motives are mixed; the Heinz Zimmermans don't. Then, when someone attacks their motives, they can get terribly hurt. They suddenly realize that they are flawed like the rest of us—ordinary human beings, and not totally admirable. And then I've seen the likes of Zimmerman lose all self-confidence. You ever heard of Venetian tears, Tom?"

"I don't think so, sir."

"They were popular toys in my childhood, globs of molten glass that had been dropped into ice-cold water. They hardened into a little hollow ball with a long, hairlike tail. They were so hard you could throw them against a wall or stomp on them or hit them with a hammer, and they wouldn't break. But snap off that little tail, and they'd shatter into dust so fine you couldn't even see the particles. That's what I've seen happen to the likes of Heinz Zimmerman when they suddenly discover that they're no different from the rest of us."

The bishop paused, and looked at his note to Zimmerman and the Xerox of Mrs. Holloway's letter which Martini had stapled onto it.

"This vile woman," he said, "doesn't give a damn for St. Jerome, of course. She only wants revenge for her husband's failure. But she managed to touch an exposed nerve. A nasty business. I don't like it one bit."

When he saw the letter addressed in a woman's hand and marked "<u>PERSONAL</u>!" in the corner—underlined, and with an exclamation mark—Jack Mulcahey almost panicked. Such letters had made his life a nightmare some years earlier.

Mulcahey had considered secretaries and shopgirls fair game, from the time he had gone to work in the Depression as manager of one of the four small shops his father owned in Capital City until, a generation later, in 1969, he had sold Mulcahey's Value Stores with its five hundred supermarkets and discount centers for a fancy price to a New York conglomerate. He had always kept these affairs casual, had never pretended to "love" any of the women or even to have much interest in them. And yet, after the sale of his company, when *Fortune* ran a story on him and called him "one of America's twenty-five richest men," he found himself inundated with letters, all in a feminine hand, all marked "<u>PERSONAL</u>" in the corner, all demanding money, threatening exposure, paternity suit, or scandal. Most of the writers withdrew hastily when his attorney pointed out that the law has an ugly word for people who demand money under threats. Altogether the episode had cost him more in lawyers' fees than in money to buy the women off.

But all his life Jack Mulcahey had been morbidly afraid of scandal, of exposure, and of derision, whether to his face or behind his back. His father had delighted in humiliating and shaming him in public when he was a little boy and wet his bed or, some years later, when he had gotten slapped in public by a girl at a junior-high-school party as he clumsily tried to put his hand down the front of her dress.

Those letters made the worst of his fears come true and upset him for months.

"But," he reassured himself, "that was ten years ago." He had not abandoned the pursuit of casual sex, and had no intention of doing so. Only now he satisfied his needs by entertaining call girls several times a week in the suite he maintained as "Mr. Gray" in Capital City's leading hotel—a different woman each time, procured for him by the door-man.

Still his hands shook slightly as he opened the envelope. One glance at the signature reassured him; there was no "Lisa Holloway" in his life and never had been. A second glance at the opening sentence, and he knew what kind of letter this was: a perfectly harmless one, the truculent whine of a fired employee, or rather, the employee's wife. Such a letter called for only one response, the wastepaper basket.

But as he began to shred the six pages into small pieces (that much at least he had learned ten years ago), his eye was caught by the one word "woman." And so he read:

. . . the President gives grave offense by sharing an office with a woman much younger than he, who is constantly in his company and who openly without even attempting discretion visits him at the President's residence most Sundays under the pretext of taking work to him. Much as it pains me, I have to submit to you, Mr. Chairman, that such conduct on the part of an ordained priest calls for a most shameful interpretation.

Mulcahey collapsed into his chair and groaned so loudly that Mrs. Gould, his old secretary, looked up sharply and almost spoke to him without first being spoken to. This was worse, far worse, than a threat to publish indiscreet letters, to sue for money allegedly promised a former girl friend, to bring a paternity suit, or even to pillory him for having debauched a fifteen-year-old virgin after luring her into his apartment and plying her with liquor—all the themes of earlier letters. Such things might have gotten him into the papers or perhaps even into court. But the charge that Father Heinz Zimmerman and his administrative assistant had a clandestine affair, if ever it became public, was all his daughters needed to try to get control of him and, above all, of his money.

Jack Mulcahey's wife—he had married her when he graduated from college forty-four years ago—would be totally indifferent to any scandal about St. Jerome University, just as she had become totally indifferent to her husband's flagrant infidelities which began as soon as they were married: he seduced their newly hired maid, a young Irish girl, ten days after returning to Capital City from their brief honeymoon. But his three daughters would make a Roman circus out of it. They resented nothing as much as his gifts to St. Jerome, feared nothing as much as that he would leave something in his will away from them and to the university. "You have no right," Jackie, the oldest, had shouted at him years ago, "to give OUR money to those no-good priests!"

Even without the trust funds he had set up for them, his daughters were very well off, each having made an excellent marriage. And yet they always wanted more. They wanted money, of course; but they even more wanted control of the money. And his gifts to St. Jerome were a constant reminder that he, not they, was in control, a constant reminder of their dependence on him, of his offense in being still alive and even active, when there was nothing he could contribute to them except his speedy demise.

Any scandal about St. Jerome, and especially a scandal involving Heinz Zimmerman, whom none of his daughters had ever met but whom all three had come to hate as the symbol of their frustration and impotence, would give them the handle they needed. Maybe they could not have their father declared legally incompetent and put under guardianship, though if they tried their mother would surely cheer them on. But they would do everything they possibly could to humiliate, deride, and ridicule him. If they ever found out that a hypocrite, an imposter, a false priest, had diddled him—no, not him, *them*—out of millions of dollars, they would hound him until he gave in and handed over the money to them, or until he left the St. Jerome board, and with it the activity he had come to enjoy the most.

Mulcahey had been hesitant when, fifteen years earlier, he had been asked to become the first layman to serve on the St. Jerome Board of Regents. Of course, it was a great honor. But though he was an alumnus of St. Jerome (he had received a Bachelor of Commerce degree in the depth of the Great Depression in the first class of the new undergraduate Business School), he had never felt at ease with professors, deans, and priests. Fifteen years later, he still much preferred the company of businessmen, such as Walter Fyneman of the department store or the Kessler brothers, Bobbie of the bank and Dannie of the insurance company, with whom he played golf on weekends and traveled during the winter to Palm Springs and Boca Raton. Jews though they were, they spoke his language and shared his interests. He could swap stories with them, and they laughed at his jokes.

Much to his surprise—"and I've no doubt the priests were equally surprised," Mulcahey had said to himself more than once—he soon found that he contributed far more to St. Jerome than his money. Obviously, the eleven million he had given over fifteen years were most welcome. But indirectly he had made even more money for the university through real-estate deals without which it would hardly have been able to expand; through successful management of endowment funds; and, perhaps most valuably by supervising architects, building plans, and contractors, and the financing of the university's building projects.

Then, after he had sold his own company and in the same

year accepted election as the university's board chairman, St. Jerome had begun to repay him. It hadn't taken him long to find out that at fifty-three he was not ready for retirement and that managing his own investments, while fun, did not keep him busy more than a day a week. The two days he gradually came to spend each week at his St. Jerome office, working closely with the university's financial and business people, came to be his real life. Once again he was doing what he did best: building rapid growth.

And now all this was in jeopardy because a fool woman was spreading slander. But was the woman (what was her name . . . Holloway?) really the problem? Or was she just hitting out in blind rage to defend the incompetent she had married? Wasn't it Heinz Zimmerman who was to blame? Not for fornication, which in any case was his own business, and that of his confessor. No, for something far more serious: imprudence.

Once in the horrible months when all those former women employees had been hounding him with their claims for money and their threats of scandal and exposure, Mulcahey had complained to his lawyer that he hadn't been doing anything hundreds of other employers weren't doing every day without any aftereffects. "Yes, Jack," the lawyer had said, "and when you did it, you were just like them. But now you are somebody highly visible. To behave like other men is worse than a crime; it's imprudent. It doesn't even matter," the lawyer had concluded, "whether you actually do the things that make you vulnerable or not. If you appear to do them, you're imprudent."

Prudence—that much Jack Mulcahey remembered from the Philosophy course he had been forced to sit through as a freshman at St. Jerome—was a cardinal virtue and Imprudence a deadly sin.

Heinz Zimmerman was surely "somebody," and highly visible. He was thus clearly guilty of gross imprudence. What did it matter that he had probably never noticed that Agnes

Muller was a beautiful woman, or even that she was a woman at all? He had no business putting himself in a compromising situation by being alone all day with a sexy-looking gal and having her come to his apartment in full view of everybody every Sunday so that a disgruntled employee could slander him and thereby endanger the university and Jack Mulcahey's peace of mind and happiness at St. Jerome.

"God only knows," thought Mulcahey to himself in horror, "how many other people she sent a similar letter to. I'm afraid it's too late to stop her, all we can do is contain the damage. I can't do much—Zimmerman isn't my subordinate. But Heinz Zimmerman is a monk; he does have a superior. It's Willy Huber's responsibility to put a stop to such imprudence. After all, it's a threat to his Order."

Of all the men on the St. Jerome Board, Mulcahey respected Willy Huber least. Huber was the very personification of the schoolmaster; though fifteen years out of the classroom (he had been principal of one of the Order's junior high schools before being elected General), Huber always looked and moved and smelled as if enveloped in a cloud of chalk dust. And he spoke with a schoolmaster's nasal falsetto, and in the measured, bored monotone of a schoolmaster dictating to the slow spellers in the class.

And then Mulcahey, the self-made man, despised Willy Huber as an also-ran. What made this so delicate in the present predicament was that it was Heinz Zimmerman who had beaten Huber in every race. The two, Mulcahey had learned long ago, were born and grew up in the same German blue-collar precinct in Milwaukee and had entered the same parochial school together. But whereas Heinz Zimmerman had become the star of his high school's championship basketball team and the toast of the neighborhood, Huber had finished as business manager of the school paper. Zimmerman had returned from World War II a captain and a much-decorated combat hero; Huber had served throughout the war as a chaplain's assistant and had come back a PFC. The Order had sent

Zimmerman upon graduation from St. Jerome to a prestigious German university to get a doctorate. Huber went to the state's Aggie college to get a master of arts in teaching. Zimmerman had become, first, a university professor, then university president; Huber had started as a language teacher in one of the Order's junior highs and then became a junior-high principal. Willy Huber even owed his election as General of the Brotherhood of St. Jerome to Heinz Zimmerman, who had thrown it to him as one throws a dog a bone when Dean Ritter, the Brothers' first and unanimous choice, had declined. "How do you at St. Jerome select your General?" Mulcahey had asked in the faculty dining room shortly after the election. "By proven incompetence, it seems," one of the older priests at the table had answered, and everyone chuckled.

Yet Willy Huber *was* Brother General and Heinz Zimmerman *was* a member of the Order. And so, with a wry grimace, Jack Mulcahey dialed Father Huber's number.

"So you, too, have received that scurrilous letter," Willy Huber said immediately. "I was just debating with myself whether I should throw it straight in the wastepaper basket or send it on to Heinz Zimmerman."

"Don't do either," Jack Mulcahey said. "Let's first think through what we should do about the allegations."

"You can't possibly take this nonsense about the anti-Catholic conspiracy at St. Jerome seriously?" asked Willy Huber incredulously.

"That's not what I mean, Father Willy," said Mulcahey, totally mystified. "It's the insinuation about Heinz Zimmerman and Agnes Muller that's bothering me."

Now it was Willy Huber's turn to be mystified, and he had to be told where to find the paragraph about Zimmerman's imprudence in his relations with Agnes Muller. "Oh that," he said; "pay no attention to it. They say that about every priest" (except those, he added to himself, whom they suspect of misconduct with boys); "no one who knows either Heinz or Mrs. Muller will believe a word of it."

"But," Mulcahey answered, quite irritated and quite sharp, "how many people *know* Heinz Zimmerman or Agnes Muller? You and I and the others on the board and the senior men in St. Jerome's administration, that's all. The rest will be only too willing to believe it. And Zimmerman's conduct almost asks to be questioned. It's been the height of imprudence. I could kick myself for not blowing the whistle sooner—and you should have done so, too. Now I think we must demand of these two that they make sure they cannot be suspected or accused. There must be no further occasion at which they are alone together and appear to have an opportunity to be intimate. Both of us have the duty to make sure of that, you as Superior of the Order, I as chairman of the Regents."

There was a long silence at the other end. "He believes," thought Mulcahey to himself, "that an accusation of sexual misconduct at this time and age isn't so very serious anymore, but being a priest doesn't dare say so. And of course, he's wrong. He doesn't know my daughters." But all Mulcahey said to break the silence was: "And what, Father Willy, do you as General of the Order propose to *do*? The least I can think of is to command Zimmerman to take the proper steps so that he isn't seen alone with Mrs. Muller at the office anymore—and she must stop coming to his home, whether there's somebody else there or not." And with that he hung up firmly.

Willy Huber sat quietly for a long time before, with a look of utter disgust at the receiver, he put it back into its cradle. "He believes this preposterous story. But maybe I shouldn't be too surprised. If one tenth of what I've heard about Jack Mulcahey is fact, he probably can't imagine that a man can be alone with a woman for more than ten minutes without bedding her. And if he believes something so utterly absurd when he's known Heinz Zimmerman for fifteen years, what won't a stranger believe? Mulcahey is coarse and vulgar, but he's shrewd and knows the world. What if he was right and there is genuine danger to the Order and the university?"

With this Huber felt anger rising in him, anger at that wretched woman, anger at Mulcahey, but above all anger at Heinz Zimmerman. "Jack Mulcahey is correct," he thought. "Heinz has been grossly imprudent. I've got to act. If there is a scandal and it hurts St. Jerome, I must be able to show that I did something."

Willy Huber had no great desire to lock horns with Heinz Zimmerman. Whenever he had done so in the past, ever since their first fight as little boys in elementary school, he had come out second-best.

Huber also had no desire to be reminded once again that all he had achieved on his own until Zimmerman had nominated him for election as General had been to teach junior high. But for all his arrogance, Heinz Zimmerman was still a St. Jerome Brother. And Willy Huber, for all that he had never gotten a Ph.D. or made the cover of *Time* magazine, was still his superior as General of the Brotherhood. So Willy Huber, sternly reminding himself of his duty, put in a call to Heinz Zimmerman.

He should have felt elated when, ten minutes later, he hung up. He had never before won against Heinz Zimmerman; at the very least he had expected a hard fight. But Heinz had given in—fast and completely.

Thank God, he had already known of the woman's letter; the Bishop, it seemed, had sent him a copy, so Huber did not have to explain why he was calling. Heinz had, of course, tried to argue: "What you want me to do, Willy," he had said when told to put a secretary from the typists' pool into one of the office rooms he shared with Agnes Muller, "is an insult to a good and decent woman."

"Your responsibility and mine," Huber had replied stiffly, "is to the Order of which Mrs. Muller is a paid employee."

Heinz had shown fight only when Huber, adding that he also spoke for Jack Mulcahey, had demanded that he not let Agnes call anymore at his residence and had overruled as irrelevant the argument that Father Ritter lived there too and was always present. "Any psychiatrist will tell you, Willy," Heinz had argued, "that you must not appease a paranoid." Then Huber had found himself saying, with great satisfaction, "You leave me no choice but to call a convocation of the Order and submit our dispute to the entire Brotherhood. If you have any regard for the good name and feelings of the lady, you wouldn't want that, I am sure." And Heinz Zimmerman had caved in.

But instead of being elated, Willy Huber was uneasy and scared. It was almost as if Zimmerman had felt guilty. Yet this was preposterous. It was not that Heinz was incapable of being attracted by a woman or of having sexual relations with her. On the contrary, the young Heinz Zimmerman had had quite a reputation as a ladykiller, so much so that at first his friends had refused to believe he had decided to enter the priesthood at the end of his first year back from the war and again at the university. What Heinz Zimmerman *was* incapable of, however, was concealment. Willy Huber had known many of Zimmerman's moods in the fifty years since they had first met in parochial kindergarten. He had known him arrogant and contentious, bullheaded and aggressive, and overbearing—but secretive, never. And it would take a master of intrigue and dissimulation to carry on an affair with Agnes Muller in full view of the entire university and living in the same house with that paragon of priestly virtue, Erwin Ritter.

What, then, was the explanation for Zimmerman's meekness when he should have charged like a wounded bull?

Heinz Zimmerman asked himself the same question after

Willy Huber finally hung up. But he knew the answer. His concern was not Huber, or Jack Mulcahey; it was Agnes.

Tuesday morning had begun with a return to normality and routine. When Agnes arrived at the office at twenty minutes past eight, the door was open, the lights were on, and Father President was standing at his desk and singing out: "Good morning, Agnes, do come in and help me sort the mail." And as she took off her coat, he looked up and said: "I hope you didn't freeze; it's beastly cold outside. But I must say the red the wind puts in your cheeks becomes you."

Then she had made breakfast for both of them and they had eaten it at the conference room table. Afterwards they had sat down across from each other at his desk and begun the day's work.

But just before she came in—he had already heard her footsteps in the hall—Heinz Zimmerman had espied a letter with the bishop's crest and address, marked "Personal" in the corner, and had, on a hunch, hastily slipped it into his pocket. He opened it an hour later when Agnes had gone off to Dean Ritter's office down the hall to fetch a potential donor's file. Inside he found Lisa Holloway's letter and the bishop's note of encouragement and support.

The Holloway letter Heinz Zimmerman shrugged off; it wasn't the first time that he had wasted his pity. But the bishop's brief words set off alarm bells in his mind.

The bishop must have known that the university could not take any action against Mrs. Holloway. She was not even an employee, and had carefully refrained from making an accusation, instead piously expressing her fear lest others might do so.

No, the note was surely meant as a warning. And the only part of the Holloway letter in which O'Malley could have detected any sort of danger was that passage about him and Agnes.

In his high-school and early college days Heinz Zimmerman, the glamorous basketball hero, had been chased by the girls and seen no reason to run away from them. He had forsworn carnal love, of course, when he entered the novitiate. But while he stayed faithful to his obligation, the recollection of his earlier sexual activities had increasingly come to make him doubt his fitness for the priesthood. Toward the end of his first year as a novice, he felt he had to make a clean breast of his sinful past to the Father Novice-Master.

"Why do you tell me all this filth?" Father Riem had asked, quite harshly.

"I thought you and the Order ought to know."

"You are a simpleton," the priest had said. "Don't you realize that we checked you out pretty carefully before we accepted you as a novice? We may not know of every girl you slept with, but we know of more than you probably remember yourself, and enough to tell us you were as much of an athlete off the field as on it.

"But, Heinz," Father Riem had continued in a warmer tone, "it's not such a bad idea for a young man who aspires to the priesthood to have known the temptations of the flesh. Then he understands what sacrifice he has to bring to become a servant of Holy Church. If he gets through the novitiate without unbearable suffering and without succumbing, he can take the vow of chastity with confidence and a good conscience."

"And that," thought Zimmerman, "is precisely how it did work out. Which is why Agnes and I can have the relationship we do.

"Of course," he mused, "I've always known that Agnes Muller is a very beautiful woman. And if I weren't a priest, it wouldn't be at all hard for me to fall in love with her. But I *am* a priest; and I learned years ago not to fall into that kind of love with a woman. I know it and Agnes knows it, and everyone else who knows either of us, even superficially, knows it too. Anyway, it would be easier to hide an elephant in my desk drawer than for Agnes and me to conceal an affair in this office where the door is always open, a hundred people troop in and out each day, and there's less privacy than at the baggage counter at Kennedy Airport with eight jumbo jets arriving at the same time."

But still the bishop must have seen a threat to Agnes to send so strong, so atypical a signal. "No one who knows us will believe the ravings of this sick woman," he thought. "Yet even in this age of women's lib, it's always the woman to whom the mud sticks."

What should he do? What could he do? He wondered whether he should tell Agnes, but knew at once that his relationship with her would never be the same were he to show her the Holloway letter. Could it be the same if he were to conceal it from her? He had never hidden anything from her, certainly not when it concerned her. What would she think if she ever found out that he had kept secret from her a letter like this, with its vile insinuations against her decency, her honesty, and her honor as a woman?

All these thoughts went through Zimmerman's head again and again as he half-mechanically sorted the papers of a proposed fund-raising drive for the Engineering School. He had almost decided to keep the letter to himself, at least until he could discuss it with Erwin Ritter after dinner in the evening, when the phone rang and Agnes said: "It's Father Willy Huber. He wants to talk to you in private."

Whatever else it did, that telephone call settled the issue of whether to tell Agnes or not. As soon as he had hung up, Zimmerman walked over to Agnes's desk, sat down on the chair beside it, and told her, first, of the Holloways' visit on Sunday and his call on Monday to Harriet Beecher Stowe. Then he gave her the two letters to read, Lisa Holloway's and the bishop's. And finally he repeated to her the orders—for they were orders—that Willy Huber and Jack Mulcahey had given them.

His mind was completely calm; he was not conscious of any emotion, not even of rage. It was also completely made up. Agnes, he was sure, would start crying—any woman would.

And he would then put his arms around her and console her. For thirty-three years, since that hour with Father Riem when he was still a novice, he had avoided physical contact with a woman. But surely the time had come for him to remember that the world called him "Father" and to start acting like one.

Of course, if anyone should see him holding Agnes sobbing in his arms there would be no need for Lisa Holloway's letter; all of St. Jerome would put the same interpretation on their relationship. "But," he thought, "I'd rather be guilty of a lack of prudence than a lack of compassion. Anyhow, it's unlikely. The desk in her corner can't be seen from the hall or until one has come right inside the door.

"I'm already infected by that horrible letter," he thought with that detachment and tendency to look at himself as if from the outside that had set him aside from his friends and playmates even as a little boy. "That's why I chose to sit at Agnes's desk rather than have her come in and sit at mine where we normally sit together, and where everyone can see us from the hall through the open door. Never mind. What matters now is Agnes, and being at her own desk might make it a little easier for her."

But Agnes had totally spoilt his script, had, indeed, totally confounded him. She listened in silence. When he told her of Willy Huber's call, she turned so pale that he was afraid she would faint. But then, just as he thought, "She's starting to cry," he saw to his utter amazement a deep blush begin at her throat and spread upward until her whole face up to the hairline glowed crimson. "Please, Father Heinz," she said, very softly but quite distinctly, "please go away and let me think for a few minutes." And when he had walked back to his own desk, quite bewildered, she got up and quietly closed the door between their offices behind him.

As soon as Father Heinz began to speak, Agnes Muller knew that her worst forebodings of yesterday had come true. It was the tone of his voice rather than what he said that told her something very serious, something irreparable, had happened to their relationship. And when he gave her the two letters, something inside her snapped. Never again, she knew, would she be unself-conscious in his presence. That woman's touch—and equally the bishop's letter, a letter she found hamhanded, patronizing, and almost contemptuous— had forever defiled what had been a pure, childlike trust, a love of brother and sister, a partnership in a common venture. Both of them, but she especially, from now on would always have to emphasize, to accent the innocence of their relations. They would forever have to stress that there was nothing between them, which could only render every word spoken between them, every gesture, every moment together rancid with suppressed sensuality.

Then, when she heard the preposterous story of Willy Huber's call and his "rules" for their future conduct, she almost died of guilt. She had a low opinion of Huber, shared, she knew, by Father Heinz; he was a fussy bureaucrat. She had an even lower opinon of Jack Mulcahey, a haberdasher's clerk for all his money, who every time they met at a board meeting or a conference tried to undress her with his eyes. That these two apes dared humiliate Father Heinz, dared gloat over him, treat him like a schoolboy caught cheating at an exam, was her fault, entirely her fault. She had exposed him, had made him vulnerable, had brought him low. And it was for her sake, she knew, that Heinz Zimmerman had submitted, had not at once called their bluff, and chased them with their tails between their legs back into the fetid holes out of which they had crawled.

"I'm old enough," she thought, "not to mind what people say about me and my morals. If I had loved a man I would not, as a widow, have had much compunction about an affair with him, even if he had been married—though I know I would never have been a priest's mistress. But that I have been the means to wound, to compromise the one person I worship, that I have failed to protect him, have endangered his mission . . . no, I can't stand it."

At that moment she had felt herself going under, and it

62

needed all her strength not to reach out and grasp Heinz Zimmerman's arm to steady herself.

But then she suddenly felt a totally different sensation, felt herself almost overwhelmed by passion and desire. "Heinz, Heinz," she wanted to cry out aloud, "why don't you take me in your arms and say, 'Let's run away together'? Why don't you at least say, 'I wish it could have been true'?" She had not felt such fierce, raw emotion since that summer's night, ages ago, when, still a few months before their wedding (indeed, even before their engagement had been officially announced), she had given herself to Jake. Suddenly she was back again behind the bushes in the park, and felt again the ecstasy and joyous pride, the guilt and even the pain—for Jake had been almost as inexperienced as she was and quite clumsy.

She was so ashamed of herself that she didn't dare look at Heinz Zimmerman. "So this horrible woman is right," she said to herself. "I am not chaste, and my relationship with Heinz Zimmerman is not what I've pretended it to be all these years."

And Marietta, her daughter, had been right too, when at sixteen in her teen-age need to hurt her mother, she had screamed: "You don't love me, you don't care one hoot about me. The only one you care for is that lover-boy of yours, that wonderful Father President!" And Sister Renée, the university's public-relations V.P., had been right too when she had called Agnes in three years ago and tried to talk her into accepting the vice presidency Heinz had offered her. "But, Renée," Agnes had argued, "I don't even have a college degree and all of you have Ph.Ds."

"Nonsense, Aggie," Renée had replied, "degrees have nothing to do with it and you know it: VP-Administration isn't an academic job. The only reason you don't want to take it is that you don't want to move out of Heinz's office, where you can see him all day long, sit next to him every working hour, and know everything he's doing or planning." She'd been so mad at Renée that she had stormed out of her office, slammed the door, and hadn't spoken to her for weeks. Yet Renée had been her closest friend since they were schoolgirls together.

Both Marietta and Renée had been right—and everybody else must have known it too, everybody but the shameless fool she'd been.

It was then she felt hot all over with a blush that was both shame and desire. "Heinz *must* see it," she thought, "and will forever fear and loathe and despise me."

But with an effort that seemed to take a whole eternity, she forced herself to speak in a quiet voice and ask him to leave her alone for a few minutes. Only after she had closed the door behind him and crept back to her corner did the tears come, hot, angry tears that gave no relief.

Fifteen minutes later she had herself under control again and went back to Heinz Zimmerman's office.

"Father Huber and Mr. Mulcahey," she said, "might have been a little more tactful; but they have a point. I should have seen it myself, and long ago. You and your work are much too important to be exposed to gossip, however groundless it is. I'll have a desk moved into the other corner of my office tomorrow and ask Mrs. Lopez—the woman in the typing pool who has been doing both your work and mine—to move in and do her typing here and answer the phone. And I'll get one of the men from Maintenance to take the work to you at the President's residence on Sundays. Maybe," and she forced a wan smile, "I can have you and Father Ritter once in a while come to my place for Sunday dinner. I daresay my cooking is better than that of the lay brothers at the residence hall."

Willy Huber woke up Wednesday morning with a throbbing headache. He had spent a miserable night tossing in his bed, until at three he had knocked himself out for a few hours of nightmare dreams with a double dose of sleeping pills.

After reporting his Tuesday morning conversation with Zimmerman to Jack Mulcahey, Willy Huber had put St. Jerome University out of his mind and gone to work on his

64

own urgent problem: the upcoming negotiations with the lay teachers at the Order's high schools, who were threatening to join a labor union unless they received raises way beyond the Order's ability to pay.

It was only after dinner that Huber again thought of Heinz Zimmerman and the morning's conversation with him. Then near-panic seized him. All of a sudden he saw a possible, indeed a highly probable, explanation for both Zimmerman's meekness and Mulcahey's alarm: that odious woman in her letter had only repeated what all of St. Jerome was already talking about. There *was* a scandal—and both Zimmerman and Mulcahey knew it. The only person who had not heard it, apparently, was he himself, the Brotherhood's General and the man responsible both to the Brothers and the hierarchy of the Church for the Order's conduct and good name. What an incompetent they must all think him!

Willy Huber knew himself to be fully qualified, perhaps even overqualified, as the Order's administrator. But even during the moment of triumph when he accepted the election to an office he had never dared aspire to, he had suffered agonies of self-doubt about his ability to give leadership in a genuine crisis. Here now was a crisis—and he didn't even know whether it really was one, or only a spiteful letter by a hysterical female that belonged in the wastepaper basket. If scandal genuinely threatened the Order's most prominent member and proudest possession, the university, what should he do?

One thing was clear to Huber. It was his duty to find out what was really going on; or rather, whether anything was really going on. But how? He had spent a sleepless night without finding an answer.

Then, as he was preparing his simple breakfast, it came to him suddenly: "Ask Foxy!" He almost shouted with relief.

Father Foxy Frantzen still had the long pointed fox's nose, but he had long ago lost most of the bushy red hair that had earned him the nickname in his student days; and what was left of it, as well as of the bristly red mustache, had long turned iron-gray. What explained the persistence of the nickname was his constant sniffing for gossip: Foxy attracted gossip as a magnet attracts steel filings. He was not malicious. He was not salacious, though he seemed to know what went on in every faculty bedroom. He did not make up tales, nor deal in gossip to make himself important. He was simply as "'satiably curious" as Kipling's Elephant Child.

Surely, Willy Huber thought, Foxy would have heard if there were even the slightest whiff of a rumor, even the slightest snicker about two such prominent and visible members of the university community as its president and his chief assistant.

"No, Willy, there's no such rumor, I am positive. I would have heard it, believe me," Foxy had responded, totally surprised.

Then Willy Huber made his great mistake—the mistake for which he was to atone three months later when, after a long session with Erwin Ritter, he announced his resignation as General of the Brotherhood "for personal reasons." Huber said: "Foxy, believe me, I'm not asking out of idle curiosity. I have a good reason, even though I can't tell you what it is. I do need to know whether there is any such gossip anywhere on campus and who is spreading it. I know you'll be discreet. Keep your ears open and let me know if you hear anything."

Willy Huber's question about Heinz Zimmerman and Agnes Muller had amused Foxy. How could anyone believe such a tale when the two were always in full view of the whole administrative staff, in an office with an open door just off the building's main entrance? But Huber's request upset Foxy. He had never seen any harm in repeating gossip. Starting it was another matter. And wasn't this what Huber had asked him to do?

Still, Huber was the General, and apparently something was going on, something dark and secret, affecting the

Order's welfare. He could not simply disregard Huber's request as he had at first meant to do. But he had to be extraordinarily careful and discreet. And it was precisely Foxy's attempts to be discreet that caused the damage.

Had Foxy gone out about the job in his normal way, had he for instance button-holed colleagues and asked point-blank: "Have you heard the latest, the silly rumor about Heinz Zimmerman and Agnes Muller?", he might have done damage to his own reputation but very little else.

But by making a big to-do, by telling everybody that he couldn't tell them why he asked, swearing them to secrecy, checking whether anyone else was listening, and, above all, by hinting rather than speaking plainly, he produced the greatest possible disturbance. "I know it isn't true," he would say to a colleague and fellow priest, "but have you heard anyone tell an odd story about an unusual relationship between a man and a woman very high up in the university? Anything of this sort?" And he asked the questions in a whisper, in a corner, or after having made carefully sure that the door was closed. He created an atmosphere of intrigue, of mystery—and the tale spread like wildfire through the small community of St. Jerome priests on campus.

Foxy himself was at first totally unaware of what he had done. On Thursday evening, thirty-six hours after Willy Huber had talked to him, he left for a conference in the East on the teaching of mathematics to undergraduates. When he returned to the priests' residence hall just in time for the Sunday evening meal, he found himself immediately surrounded and besieged, mainly of course by the younger men. "Is it true, Foxy, that you have a choice story to tell?" an assistant professor of classics greeted him. "Foxy," another asked, "what is this I hear about a scandal in the Administration Building?" And, "Have you heard, Foxy, that the Brother General has ordered an investigation very high up?"

Foxy fled, leaving his dinner uneaten. He ran straight to Erwin Ritter, caught him just as he was going to bed, and poured out the story. Ritter knew about Lisa Holloway's letter, Willy Huber's telephone call, and Agnes's decision to accede to Huber's request; Heinz Zimmerman had gone to him shortly after his talk with Agnes. But he had no inkling of Huber's subsequent call to Foxy, nor of the uproar among the faculty. His closest friend would never have dared repeat gossip to Erwin Ritter.

Ritter sternly ordered Foxy to keep his mouth shut. "If anyone asks you anything about the rumor, you tell him to come to me." But that only heightened the mystery, ensuring that all the priests became convinced something momentous was going on. Anyone who did go to Ritter—and many of the older men who had known him for years did so—got a stern lecture about spreading slander and the wickedness of even mentioning something so palpably absurd and cruelly vicious, with strict instructions to discipline any junior who might indulge in loose talk. And, as he hadn't done for years, Erwin Ritter took to having his supper in the refectory of the priests' residence instead of in his own rooms in the house next door he shared with Heinz Zimmerman. There, his silence and his grim looks dared anyone to as much as mention the subject.

But making it taboo only convinced his colleagues, and especially the younger men, to whom both Heinz Zimmerman and Agnes Muller were remote names rather than flesh-and-blood people with whom they had worked closely, that there must be something going on. What, no one quite knew—few believed in an illicit love affair; it was obviously quite impossible for those two ever to have been together where they wouldn't be seen and observed by countless eyes. Yet surely something terribly important, terribly serious, must be happening. Why otherwise these attempts to hush things up? Where at first a good many of the priests had shouted, they now began to whisper. Where they had talked openly, they now began to argue in corners, often heatedly, only to break off and turn silent the moment someone else approached. Where they had at first treated the whole thing as a joke, albeit one in very dubious taste (but then Foxy wasn't much noted for his taste, anyhow), they now began to be afraid.

Erwin Ritter soon realized that he had done the worst thing. But there was no one with whom he could discuss the matter. He surely could not mention it to Heinz with whom, for almost thirty years, he had talked out every problem at St. Jerome. He could not discuss it with the chairman of the Regents or the General of the Order, even if he had had greater respect for either Mulcahey or Huber.

Then he thought of Seymour Bercovitz and decided to pay him a visit.

Bercovitz was Heinz Zimmerman's friend rather than Ritter's. But Ritter had seen enough of the doctor to have come to like him and have confidence in his judgment. And what was going on at St. Jerome seemed to Ritter to call for a psychiatrist's knowledge and advice.

"You are quite right, Father Dean," said Dr. Bercovitz. "What you are faced with at the university falls within our province. It sounds to me suspiciously like an attack of mass hysteria, though a fairly mild one. I know laymen think that's an affliction of women, and mainly adolescent ones. But that's a misunderstanding. Hysteria is equally common to both sexes and has nothing to do with age. It's a kind of emotional epidemic—and highly contagious. It typically occurs in small, self-contained, rather isolated communities where there is considerable emotional tension, with conflicts being suppressed in the subconscious" ("And what greater tension," Bercovitz added to himself, "could there be among today's young Catholic priests than worry about sex and celibacy? They must hear every day of one of their colleagues leaving the priesthood to get married.")

"There is no known treatment and no known cure," he went on. "In the old days one called in the priest, who tried exorcism. It rarely worked. Now you call in the psychiatrist, who talks learnedly about suppression and sublimation and psychic dynamics and drives. That doesn't work, either. Fortunately, mass hysteria usually takes care of itself, and pretty fast. I won't pretend that it's no worse than the common cold; it can do a lot of damage. And it's very painful, as you've found out, but so is a pebble in the shoe. Usually it burns itself out within a few weeks. There is only one thing that must be avoided, one thing that can make it dangerous. It's really the oldest media event around and feeds on attention, publicity, and speechmaking. Just treat it with neglect and amused tolerance. Laughter, believe me, and being made light of, are the two things mass hysteria cannot survive.

"The important point to make sure of for you at the university," Bercovitz concluded, "is that your senior men, the department chairmen and deans and distinguished older faculty, keep cool heads and go about their normal business as if nothing out of the ordinary were happening. That shouldn't be too difficult, I trust."

Erwin Ritter assured the psychiatrist that, indeed, it shouldn't be difficult at all. But he left Bercovitz's office with considerable forebodings. In his own heart he was by no means sure that the senior men at St. Jerome would have the self-discipline to go about their business as usual and give Heinz Zimmerman and the university their unquestioning support. Some of them, he was very much afraid, were busy blowing up a storm of their own. And once again the Holloways were at the center of this second turbulence.

PART THREE

When Clem Boglund returned to his office on Monday afternoon from a luncheon meeting with his senior chemistry professors, he found Philip Oberhumer, the chairman of Earth Sciences, waiting for him. "Can I see you for a few minutes in private?" Oberhumer asked.

Oberhumer had been one of Heinz Zimmerman's "coups." Highly distinguished among the country's oil geologists and the holder of an endowed chair at a famous Eastern university, he had become available to St. Jerome only because his wife, Patricia Dunn, then a psychology teacher at a college near Boston, would not accept deanship at Harriet Beecher Stowe unless a first-rate job in Capital City could be found for her husband. Zimmerman had seen his opportunity and seized it. Oberhumer could not resist the offer St. Jerome had made him: no teaching duties except for the supervision of a few doctoral candidates, a substantially higher salary, and full freedom to do all the consulting work he wanted.

Oberhumer for his part had done very well by St. Jerome. He had built a strong department, which attracted first-rate young faculty. He got the cream of the country's doctoral students in his own field—and they got top jobs in industry and teaching immediately upon graduation. He also brought St. Jerome a good deal of oil money. Indeed, the oil millionaire with whom Heinz Zimmerman was having lunch that very same Monday and from whom he hoped to get enough money for a new Earth Sciences building and for three endowed professorships in geology, geophysics, and petroleum engineering, respectively, was one of Oberhumer's satisfied clients and had been brought by him to St. Jerome.

But Oberhumer was also the faculty's leading trouble-maker. At every meeting of the Chairman's Council—the university's most powerful committee and the final arbiter in most matters of academic policy and curriculum—he would bore one half to death with his impassioned tirades on "University constitution" and against "tyrannical administrators." In particular, he railed against what he called "administrative arrogance in the American university." "Instead of a president, vice presidents, and deans in battalion strength," he would declaim, "all a university needs is one clerk to make sure that the paperwork gets done and the salary checks go out on time. The rest should be run by the senior faculty, the full professors, who elect rectors and deans for short periods (three years maximum) and who alone make all decisions. Anything else is usurpation of faculty authority and results in control of science and scholarship by the vested interests, and especially the moneybags."

Oberhumer was not particularly popular with his colleagues, least of all with Boglund, whom he had once openly sneered at as "Zimmerman's tame poodle." Boglund was therefore quite surprised to find Oberhumer at his doorstep, but could hardly refuse to give him a few minutes.

"Tell me, Clem," Oberhumer began. "Who is Martin Holloway?"

"An incompetent assistant professor in my department," Boglund replied, much surprised; "an older man whom Heinz Zimmerman ordered us to hire three years ago. Otherwise, Heinz said, we'd be guilty of discrimination by age. I never thought he'd work out. And now my faculty has voted unanimously not to reappoint him."

"That's what I thought," said Oberhumer, "and that's what I told my wife."

"Why should Pat be interested?" asked Boglund, mystified.

"It's a weird story, and the only thing I can figure out is that our sneaky administration is once again trying to whittle down faculty rights. Pat called just before lunch. Her president—you've met Louise McCollough, I think—apparently got a phone call from Zimmerman this morning suggesting she hire Holloway."

"You must be making it up," said Boglund. "I can't believe it. Zimmerman knows nothing about the man except that we unanimously recommended not to reappoint him and consider him totally unfit for college teaching."

"You better believe it, Clem," said Oberhumer. "That's exactly the kind of game administrators will play unless the faculty clips their wings. Anyhow, Mrs. McCollough asked Pat to find out who this Holloway is and what goes on. After all, university presidents don't as a rule try to find jobs for fired assistant professors."

"I still can't understand it," said Boglund. "If Heinz Zimmerman sees any problem in letting Holloway go, why doesn't he bring it up with me? After all, I would have to recommend the fellow before any college hires him—and I sure couldn't do it. You can tell that to Pat. Actually, I've lined up a few industry offers for Holloway. That's where he belongs."

"You take much too relaxed a view of this, Clem," said Oberhumer. "It's a slap in your face. You and your faculty unanimously declare the man unfit, and then the President, who knows nothing about him, disavows you behind your back and recommends him for a teaching job. If that's not a declaration of nonconfidence in you and your faculty—and in all of us chairmen—I don't know what it is."

"Phil," protested Boglund, "you exaggerate. I admit that I'm stunned. Nothing like this has happened to me in my whole academic career. But I know Heinz Zimmerman. There must be some explanation, though I'm damned if I can figure it out."

"Don't be naive, Clem. There's an explanation all right. Our precious President doesn't give a fig for the rights of the faculty and never will if we let him get away with his little games. Maybe you don't want to make an issue out of it, but I shall. I'll bring it up at the next Chairmen's Council meeting two weeks from today. I think it's an outrage and an open attack on all of us chairmen and the senior faculty we represent."

Boglund didn't wait two weeks. As soon as Oberhumer had left, he phoned Erwin Ritter. And when Ritter said that he knew nothing about a telephone call about Holloway to Harriet Beecher Stowe, Boglund called Zimmerman and made an appointment to see him Wednesday morning.

Clement Boglund was not a very observant person, and he had not been in the president's office often enough to know its routine. But even he sensed immediately on Wednesday morning that something was amiss. Agnes Muller, instead of greeting him with her usual warm smile, barely nodded to him. She seemed distracted, and Boglund thought her face and eyes were swollen as if she had been crying. In one corner of the office a sour-looking middle-aged woman was exchanging angry words with a crew from Maintenance who were pushing furniture around. And Zimmerman himself seemed very different from his usual courteous and genial self. He didn't inquire after Boglund's health or his wife and children, nor about affairs in the Chemistry Department. He didn't even offer Boglund a seat.

"What's the matter, Clem?" he asked curtly. "Try to make it brief. I'm busy."

"Yes," he said, after Boglund had put his question. "I did call Louise McCollough on Monday and mentioned Holloway to her. Did Erwin Ritter tell you that he and his wife came to see me Sunday afternoon—uninvited, to be sure—and asked me to overrule you and your faculty and renew his contract? Of course I said no. But I felt sorry for the fellow, he was so totally crushed. And then I remembered that Louise McCollough had told me some weeks ago that she needs science teachers who have the full academic credentials but are willing to teach—and teach conscientiously—at the high-school level. I'm sorry if you feel I by-passed you; I didn't intend to. I just thought I might help a poor devil and a neighboring school as well."

"I don't understand, Heinz," Boglund said with considerable heat. "The entire faculty in Chemistry declares this man unfit to teach college courses and you, who know nothing about him or about chemistry, overrule us and recommend him for a teaching position. Don't you have any respect for our judgment or confidence in me? You know I consider it my duty as chairman to look after my faculty. If you don't trust my doing so, you better tell me so and get yourself another chairman."

"Clem," said Heinz Zimmerman in an angry voice that Boglund had never heard before, "you are making a mountain out of a molehill. If I hurt you, I'm sorry and I apologize. But I won't apologize for my phoning. It was nothing but an attempt in ordinary charity to help a fellow man in distress, and I'd do it again."

And Zimmerman all but turned his back on Boglund, staring at the wall on which his honorary doctorates were hanging. Always before he had been friendly, courteous, and had given Boglund his full attention. Now he didn't even listen.

So Boglund left, baffled. What had gotten into the man? But he was also hurt, upset, and very, very angry. "Is Oberhumer right, after all?" he asked himself as he walked across the campus. He had always scoffed at Oberhumer's rantings. Now all of a sudden he made sense to Boglund in his distrust of "Administration" and his hostility toward it.

Hiring Clem Boglund as the first department chairman who was not a priest had been one of Heinz Zimmerman's early moves upon his appointment as acting president and a giant step toward his "first-rate Catholic university."

Boglund had been barely thirty then, an associate professor

at Minnesota and a newly appointed one at that. But he was already known as a "comer." He had never heard of Heinz Zimmerman, of course, and St. Jerome was barely even a name to him. If he thought of moving at all, he thought of Stanford, where his former teacher had recently gone. But he himself had been an undergraduate, and a deeply dissatisfied one, at a Catholic university. And so when, by sheer accident, he had come across a speech this Father Zimmerman had made about the American Catholic University of the Future, he felt moved to sit down and pour out his own thoughts in a long letter. At most, he expected a polite acknowledgment. Instead, a telephone call came ten days later. "I am Heinz Zimmerman. I'll be in Minneapolis the week after next and would like to discuss your exciting letter." And at the end of their dinner Zimmerman had said, "I want you to come to St. Jerome and start doing the things your letter talks about."

Boglund had no regrets about choosing St. Jerome over Stanford. Professionally, he could not have done better. St. Jerome had been generous with lab equipment and research assistants and even with time. Boglund had managed to publish fourteen major research papers in his seventeen years at St. Jerome; and the big text on organic metallic compounds on which he had already been working in Minnesota was published five years after his move to St. Jerome, immediately became the standard work in the field, and had recently been reissued in a new and much-enlarged third edition. Meanwhile he had, indeed, built up a strong and nationally recognized Chemistry Department.

But, as Boglund knew well, his strength at St. Jerome rested less on his achievements in his own field and department than on his being the "bridge"—trusted, accepted, and followed in both camps—between the "new breed" of lay chairmen and that of the "cliff dwellers," the priests and nuns in departmental chairs. There was no open enmity between the two groups; but still they saw themselves as different, as competing, and as representing opposed, if not mutually incompatible, values and aspirations. Both, however, accepted and trusted Boglund; the one because Oberhumer tended to follow his lead, the other one because of his close friendship with Father Dennis Levecque.

Oberhumer's values, or rather, the man's total lack of values, Boglund could not abide. Boglund himself, although he had not realized it at the time, had chosen St. Jerome in preference to the prestige and glamour of Stanford in large part because, as a Catholic school, he expected it to be less corrupted by commercialism and less compromised by the embrace of industry. He passionately believed in academia's total divorce from mammon and in the scholar's single-minded dedication to the pursuit of knowledge rather than the pursuit of profit. "There is pure science and applied science," he was fond of saying, "and both are needed. But there is also pure science and impure science—and impure science no more belongs in academe than the money changers belonged in the Temple at Jerusalem." Or, "I have nothing against business and businessmen; but I am a scientist. And business and science are like eating and sleeping. You need both, but they don't mix."

And here was this Oberhumer, who freely admitted that he had chosen St. Jerome largely because it put no restrictions on his consulting work for industry, who boasted openly that his research was paid for by industry and was directed toward its needs, that, indeed, he aligned it deliberately with the research programs of the most bloated of fat cats, the oil companies. What irked Boglund the most was that Oberhumer was not a bit apologetic. On the contrary, he asserted loudly that sound theory and pure knowledge in science were most likely to result from wrestling with the problems of industry, and he had his own research achievements and those of his students to point to as proof of this detestable doctrine.

Yet in everything that really mattered—curriculum or educational policies or standards, even staffing and organization—Oberhumer always followed Boglund's lead. He made his silly speech attacking administration in general and St. Jerome's administration in particular, then voted the way Boglund had indicated he'd vote, which practically always was the straight administration ticket. And the other lay chairmen would duly fall into line behind Oberhumer.

Boglund found no such agreement on policy matters with the "cliff dwellers," nor did he expect it. They were nostalgic for the days when all chairmen were St. Jerome priests, and tended to resent him as the symbol of that new order in which St. Jerome was no longer "their" unversity. All of them—the two nuns who headed departments as well as the priests holding chairmanships—had serious reservations about a good many of Heinz Zimmerman's ideas, policies, and appointments, even though they could not find cogent rational arguments against them. Yet they accepted Clement Boglund as a person, trusted him, worked with him. And the main reason was his close friendship with one of them, Father Dennis Levecque, the chairman of Economics.

The friendship had begun on Boglund's first trip to St. Jerome, well before he had accepted the appointment, when Dennis and he discovered, sitting by accident at the same table at lunch, that they both came from the iron-mining country of northern Michigan and that their fathers, though at different times, had actually been working for the same mining company, one as electrician, the other in truck maintenance. The two of them, having grown up in the North Woods and as outdoorsmen, began to go cross-country skiing together in the winter and fishing in the summer on a remote island close to the Canadian border which could be reached only by canoe and on which Levecque owned a primitive shack.

But what kept them friends were their common values. For all their policy differences—and these were sharp—they were as one in what they thought essential. Boglund was a moderate, Levecque an extremist; but that was a matter of temperament rather than of conviction. Levecque was as firmly committed as Boglund to "keeping the money changers out of the Temple," that is, to the total divorce of academia and business, and indeed of academia and the false values and vanities of a secular, profit-seeking possession-loving society altogether. Levecque saw himself first as a priest of the Church. Boglund saw himself as a secular scientist. But both believed in the motto, *Ad majorem Dei gloriam*, which the first president of St. Jerome almost a century ago had had chiseled over the mock-Gothic portal of the Administration Building.

And they were both being defeated.

Every day Boglund saw new evidence of the enemy's advance. One after another the science departments of St. Jerome—first Biology, then Physics, finally the mathematicians—joined Oberhumer in the worship of the golden calf and the brazen pursuit of consulting assignments in industry, research contracts from business and corporation fellowships. But Boglund at least had some control over his own Chemistry Department. Control of Economics had already passed to commercialism and big business.

Dennis Levecque was a labor economist and an acknowledged expert on white-collar unions. He was active as adviser and counselor to labor leaders, most of them of the "progressive" persuasion. When the legislature had passed a law drafted by Levecque, which permitted state employees to unionize and to bargain collectively, Levecque had become Labor's appointee on the State Labor Commission. Levecque was a colorful speaker who loved the limelight and courted the press. At a time when even supposedly "radical" labor leaders had come to talk about such bloodless things as "cost/benefit ratios," "cost of living," and "productivity," Levecque's fiery, old-fashioned, "give 'em hell" rhetoric was in high demand and made excellent copy.

Needless to say, the business leaders of Capital City were not exactly enchanted by headlines such as: ST. JEROME ECONOMICS CHAIRMAN CALLS FOR NATIONALIZATION OF BIG

COMPANIES. But their opposition to Levecque got nowhere until the Graduate School of Management was founded and had begun to grow fast. As the dean of the new school soon found out, Dennis Levecque as chairman of Economics and in control of the economics taught throughout the university, including the School of Management, was a major liability in recruiting students, placing graduates, and soliciting money.

"Economics," Levecque maintained, "is a moral discipline. Its goal is a better, a more just, a more Christian society. The 'moderns,' the quantifiers with their wonderful techniques, prostitute economics. Since the only thing that can be quantified is a model of the stock market, the stock market becomes their ideal of a just economy and they become servants of corporate capitalism at its worst." And so Levecque, as chairman of Economics, pushed the old-fashioned courses: Labor Economics, Government Control of Business, Economic History, and History of Economic Thought.

"But this isn't Economics," said the Management people. "If St. Jerome wants to teach these things, put them into Philosophy or Social Science or History—but we do need real Economics." And when Levecque wouldn't budge, they played their trump card: they got the Association of Collegiate Schools of Business to suspend St. Jerome's full accreditation "pending the establishment of an adequate program in Economics."

Of course, Levecque could not be deprived of the chairmanship. The St. Jerome priests on the faculty would have revolted. What the Management people proposed was even more humiliating: to have two departments of Economics, with the new one, headquartered in Management, in control of everything except the introductory freshman courses and the seminars in Economic Policy (by which was meant only one course, the seminar in Labor Economics Levecque himself taught to a handful of students). All Boglund could accomplish—and even that almost foundered on the last-ditch resistance of the Management School—was a lame compromise: the department remained officially unsplit, with Levecque the only "Economics Chairman" at St. Jerome. But a "subdepartment" of "Managerial Economics and Statistics" was set up in the Management School with responsibility for Economics in all professional schools: Undergraduate Business, Law School, Graduate Management, and Engineering, and for quantitative and analytical courses throughout the university.

It wasn't much of a compromise, but it saved Levecque's face and that of the "cliff dwellers." Dennis was almost pathetically grateful. And the senior "cliff dweller," Father Carstens, chairman of Religion and, after Erwin Ritter, the most respected St. Jerome priest, had come in person to Boglund's office to tell him how much he appreciated what Clem had done.

All this went through Clement Boglund's mind as he fought his way against a bitter wind toward his own office at the other end of the campus. Heinz Zimmerman had hurt him deeply. And yet he couldn't see himself accepting Oberhumer's position. "I need to talk this out with someone. Why not Dennis? He usually laughs at the things that bother me, especially administrative worries. But he knows how much my responsibility for my faculty means to me and he shares my concern."

To Boglund's amazement, Dennis Levecque did not laugh. "Of course, Clem," he said, "the incident in itself is trivial. But it's far from trivial as a symptom of what's wrong with St. Jerome. It shows you how far we have gone toward the 'imperial presidency.' Forget his being rough; that's unimportant. Heinz isn't, usually, we both know that. But his going over your head and disavowing you in respect to that incompetent you're letting go—that's something else again. It shows that Zimmerman wants to have it both ways. If St. Jerome is indeed the 'first-rate university' he is forever talking about, the President has no business interfering with faculty. But the moment it pleases him, he's running St. Jerome with the personal authority of an old-fashioned religious superior. He can't have it both ways.

"Are you going to bring it up at the Chairmen's Council meeting in two weeks, Clem?"

Boglund shook his head. "I don't know yet, though I doubt it. But Oberhumer surely will."

"And Phil will make the most of it," said Levecque. "I think I'd better discuss this on Friday with the Twelve Apostles."

In its pre-Zimmerman days, St. Jerome had had twelve academic departments, all chaired by St. Jerome Fathers. By now the number of departments had almost doubled—to twenty-three—and only eight of them were chaired by religious, and two of those (Modern Languages and Journalism) by a "chairperson," one of the Sisters of St. Mary in the Plains rather than a priest. Still, the nickname of "the Twelve Apostles" hung on, as did the custom of the remaining eight lunching together at the Faculty Club every Friday at a table of their own.

On the Friday after his talk with Clem Boglund, Father Dennis Levecque carried his tray toward the table where the Twelve Apostles seemed to be having a heated argument, everybody leaning forward and whispering. But when he slid into the seat he always occupied, between Fred Carstens, chairman of Religion, and Piet Boerhave, chairman of Philosophy, everyone immediately stopped talking.

"So you, too, are gossiping about Heinz Zimmerman and Agnes Muller," he said in a bantering voice to Father Carstens.

Carstens was not amused. "You know better than that, Dennis," he said in a tone of irritation that was quite unusual for that serene man. "I leave gossiping to Foxy; he does enough of it for all of us. I am appalled though by the way everybody else is gossiping, and especially the younger priests. Twenty years ago we wouldn't have dignified such a mean little piece of dirt with a moment's attention. Now all the young priests are chattering about it like a bunch of hysterical schoolgirls discussing the sex life of a movie starlet. If that's what being a first-rate university means, give me a kindergarten any time.

"Last night I heard two of our younger priests telling each other that this absurd rumor shows how ill-advised it is of Rome not to permit priests to marry."

"You're quite right, Fred," said the chairman of classics, who as the youngest of the group both in years and seniority always felt called upon to defend the younger generation. "It's been a miserable week. But Foxy's rumor, it seems to me, has only uncovered how low morale is among the St. Jerome priests here. It hasn't been the cause. And frankly I do think that those young priests you overheard have a point. After all, there are married priests in perfectly respectable rites within the church—the Ukrainians with their Greek-Catholic Rite, for instance. Why can't Rome accept an American Rite and give us the freedom to choose our own observances in matters that do not concern Faith or Doctrine but purely discipline?"

As the Classics chairman had intended, both Carstens and Boerhave, champions of tradition and guardians of orthodoxy at St. Jerome, immediately rose to the bait. To stop them before they could launch into the set speeches everybody at the table had heard a dozen times before, Dennis Levecque intervened hastily: "Hold it. I came here with something important, something that we ought to think about"—and he told them of his talk with Clem Boglund two days earlier. "When Oberhumer makes an issue out of Heinz Zimmerman's running around Boglund—and mind you, I'm saying 'when' not 'if'; I'm sure he'll bring it up and make it sound like the crime of the century—are we going to support the administration?"

"Isn't this purely a matter between the lay faculty and the administration of which we should stay clear?" asked Sister Malvina, chairperson of Journalism, who was known to consider the Council meetings a waste of time anyway and who used very un-nunlike terms—"intellectual masturbation," for example—to express what she thought of most of the issues and problems that engaged the Council's time and attention. But Sister Malvina made far too much sense for anyone to pay attention to her.

Tall and angular, Sister Malvina was not noted for flights of fancy; totally unsentimental and without imagination, she was known as "Madam Facts" among Journalism faculty and students. But when a few weeks later she talked of the luncheon meeting of the Twelve Apostles to Tom Martini, whom the bishop had sent to find out what was going on at St. Jerome, she broke down and sobbed. "It was hateful, hateful," she said. "I felt like part of a lynch mob."

"Oh, it began quietly enough," she continued. "'I hope, Dennis,' Father Carstens said, 'that you told Clem Boglund not to pay attention to Heinz Zimmerman's rudeness. We all know—and Boglund must know it too by now—that Zimmerman was terribly upset that morning. What really goes on there, I don't know, but it must have something to do with that malicious rumor Foxy has been spreading.'

"Father Levecque assured Father Carstens that that was precisely what he had said to Professor Boglund. 'But,' he went on, 'I also told Clem Boglund that the incident and Father Zimmerman's interference on behalf of that incompetent chemist were a serious matter, if only as a symptom of the confusion St. Jerome suffers from in respect to its role and that of faculty and administration.'

"And that's when the shit hit the fan. The first one to scream—and I do mean scream—was Father Wydling, the chairman of Classics. 'That's just the way all of us have been treated,' he shouted, hammering the table with his fist. 'When Beatrice [that, said Sister Malvina, is Sister Beatrice, who chairs Modern Languages] and I went to Ritter and Zimmerman to protest against the abolition of the language requirement, they didn't even listen to us. Mind you, we didn't ask them to restore the old rule under which a student had to have both one year of Latin and one year of a modern language although both of us believe that that's a minimum. All we asked them was to keep some language requirement—and they wouldn't even listen! Zimmerman said, "We have a hard enough time getting good students to apply to St. Jerome and have to be competitive in our requirements. No respect at all for what's right, for educational values and tradition, nothing but commercial considerations.'

"Then Sister Beatrice chimed in: 'I call it meretricious, and then Felix Wydling and I get criticized because enrollments in our departments are dropping. We have a right, I'd say, to expect the President of a Catholic university to stand up for a true liberal education and not throw us to the wolves just to be trendy.'

"'And he doesn't treat Economics any differently,' Father Levecque said, and I noticed his hands were trembling with rage. Then Father Boerhave, who is usually so quiet, broke in and bellowed: 'But things are even worse in appointments and the administration is even more highhanded. It's a shame and a disgrace how in a Catholic university, one that belongs to and is run by an Order, priests are discriminated against and told we aren't good enough and don't measure up. They put a dean in at the Law School who isn't even a Catholic and pass over the priest who's been associate dean for eight years. And they put a layman into the chair of the biggest department, English, though there are eleven qualified priests and sisters among the department's faculty. And I don't know,' he went on, turning to Father Boninger, 'why we stood still when they closed down your School of Education, making it a mere department and demoting you from dean to department chairman. I know they pleaded falling enrollments, but we shouldn't have let them bamboozle us!'"

"I know, Father Martini," Sister Malvina finished up, "it all sounds petty—and it was. But I make it sound orderly and rational and at worst peevish. In fact, it was wild and vicious.

They were screaming, really screaming—the whole faculty dining room stared at our table as though we'd gone mad, and, of course, we had. I tried to remind them that every one of these measures—the abolition of the language requirements, the reorganization of the Economics Department, and the change in Education from a separate school to a department—had been discussed endlessly in the Council and carried by an overwhelming majority. Dropping the language requirement was recommended unanimously by a faculty committee. As I recall, the only ones voting to keep it were Father Wydling and Sister Beatrice. But they didn't want to hear me, they wanted to hate. They glared at me, and for a moment I thought one of them might strike me, they were so full of hatred and meanness and self-pity.

"I don't know what would have happened if Father Carstens, who was more shaken than I've ever seen him, and he's usually so unflappable, hadn't said: 'It's one-thirty and our rule is to adjourn now. Some of us have classes or appointments.' But it took him quite some time to get them to stop shouting at each other and cursing the administration.

"I know one table," Sister Malvina concluded, "where I shan't eat lunch anymore, Friday or any other day of the week."

It had been known as the "Academic Council" for a full ten years now, but it was still the "Chairmen's Council" for everyone but Erwin Ritter. The monthly meetings were indeed attended as a rule only by the chairmen and chairwomen of the twenty-three university-wide academic departments.

But when Phil Oberhumer rose on a blustery February afternoon to make an issue out of Heinz Zimmerman's telephone call to Harriet Beecher Stowe on behalf of Martin Holloway, he faced a full house. In addition to the "chairs," all seven professional-school deans were in attendance; even the three deans of the Health Care schools were there, who rarely set foot on the main St. Jerome Campus as their offices were downtown in St. Clare Hospital, nine miles away. The dean of the undergraduate liberal arts college was there, of course. But so too was the director of the Advanced Institute of Theoretical Physics, the distinguished scientist Jerry Ashenbach, who had never before in his eight years at St. Jerome shown up at a Council meeting.

There was only one absentee: the president. Heinz Zimmerman had refused to come, despite Erwin Ritter's repeated urgings. "If I show up," he had said, "everyone will know that I've come because of Oberhumer's attack—and it isn't even on the agenda. They'll expect me to apologize or to defend myself. I won't do either." And when Ritter, a few days later, tried again, Heinz Zimmerman grew petulant, said, "I'm busy," and walked out.

But what bothered Ritter most was not Zimmerman's words. It was the way they were said: listlessly, and in a tone of resignation, almost defeat.

Outwardly, there seemed to be no change in Heinz Zimmerman, and he kept to his daily routine. He had not lost his golden touch, had, for instance, without apparent effort, gotten Oberhumer's oil millionaire to pledge himself to a huge matching grant for half the cost of both a new earth sciences building and three new earth sciences professorships—far more than the donor had ever dreamed of giving, and almost twice what Zimmerman himself had expected to get when he first started courting the oilman. When he chaired meetings, Zimmerman was as courteous and considerate as ever, though, Ritter thought, one saw very little these days of the famous Zimmerman smile with its infectious warmth.

Yet to Erwin Ritter's eyes and ears there was something terribly wrong here, something terribly contrived. Zimmerman's heart simply wasn't in what he was doing, no matter how well he did it.

Ritter had known Zimmerman for forty years, since his own first week as a college teacher and Heinz Zimmerman's first week as a college freshman. During one of the very first discussion sessions of "Philosophy 101: Introduction to Logic and Philosophy," Ritter had realized that this huge, handsome, outgoing basketball player was a brilliant intellect with a searching mind, but also that this mind had never been challenged, never been disciplined, never been taught. When the young philosophy instructor returned to his room that evening, totally exhausted but also exhilarated as never before, he had gone down on his knees to thank the Lord for making him a teacher, and to pray for the strength to meet the challenge of the likes of Heinz Zimmerman. And when he got up from his prayer, he thought he heard a voice within him speak the words with which Our Lord on the Cross commended his favorite disciple to his Mother: "This is Your Son."

Fifteen years later, when he had wanted to make Zimmerman assistant dean, he had to convince an elderly and very conservative president who thought the young professor of logic "far too radical" and "full of half-baked notions."

"But Zimmerman," Ritter had argued, "is himself the best proof of his thesis that Catholic colleges in the United States must change radically. In all my years of teaching I've never encountered a more brilliant student, one more eager to learn and one who so fully exemplifies St. Augustine's dictum: *Anima est naturaliter Christiana* (The soul is Christian by nature). Yet when he arrived here, after twelve years of the best education American Catholic schools can supposedly provide, his mind had never been put to work, challenged, permitted to ask a question, touched, or inspired. All he had been allowed to learn were a few phrases of the Catechism, any number of vulgar terms for the private parts of men and women, and how to throw a basketball."

Erwin Ritter had been under Zimmerman's spell from the first day they met; but he had always had one serious reservation. Heinz Zimmerman, he thought, far too much loved a fight. He was what Ritter's Austrian-born grandmother used to call a *"Raufhansl,"* a tavern brawler. Again and again in the years when Ritter was carefully grooming the younger man for higher office, he'd find himself saying: "Why can't you learn, Heinz, that one catches flies with honey?" Zimmerman's instinctive reaction was to hit out at whoever opposed him or stood in his way.

Now, it seemed, all the *Raufhansl* had gone out of him. Ritter would have expected him to be fighting mad. Instead, Heinz had become mulish, stubborn, and passive.

Ritter once more sought out Seymour Bercovitz. But the psychiatrist had no explanation. "I've noticed it, too," he said, "and so did my children when he came to the house the other evening for our weekly chess game. My daughter, she's very fond of Father Heinz, spotted it and asked me after he left whether I thought he was sick or in pain. In fact, Dean Ritter, I was tempted to call up and ask what ails Father Heinz."

"You know, doctor," Ritter replied, choosing his words carefully, "I cannot see anything that would explain Heinz being frightened or ashamed—and yet that's the way he acts. He is used to fights in the faculty; in fact, he enjoys them. To be sure, he must be annoyed at that stupid story about him and Agnes Muller, and in his shoes, I'd be so angry with those two heroes, the chairman of the Regents and the Brother General, that I'd have told them what they can do with my job. But he acts as if there were some shameful secret, some hidden wound. Yet all that's happened is a spiteful letter. And, as I told him," Bercovitz added, "a letter from a very sick woman who is hardly rational."

The evening before the Council meeting, Ritter had tried once more. He had gotten Heinz to promise to reconsider. But when the meeting opened, Zimmerman wasn't there.

Oberhumer, Erwin Ritter thought, was beginning to lose his audience.

He had started out with full-blown Ciceronian oratory.

"It is my duty, Father Dean," he had begun, "to bring before the Academic Council an incident which, while perhaps none too important in itself, raises profound and disturbing questions of academic freedom and university constitution; an incident which threatens to undermine the confidence faculty must have in the university's administration. Yes, I know, the Holloway incident is only that, an incident. But it constitutes a gross violation of the rights of department chairpersons and bespeaks a dangerous lack of trust in the integrity and judgment of the department chairman—and, above all, a lack of clarity regarding the role and functions of both administration and faculty and its chairpersons, which augurs ill for the future of this great university."

This was far too dramatic for the prosaic Academic Council at St. Jerome. But it made everyone sit up. Jerry Ashenbach, for instance, had been slumped in his chair half asleep. But when Oberhumer began, he jerked upright as if stabbed with a cattle prod. And one of the health-care deans who had been equally somnolent was heard to whisper to the other two: "Now I know why Ritter insisted we come."

But as soon as he had everyone's attention, Oberhumer turned icy calm.

"As an isolated incident, the Holloway episode wouldn't matter, but it isn't an isolated incident. Unfortunately, it's but the latest in a long series of similar events, each showing that the administration is confused about its role—and about our role as well. Whether this results from a lack of clarity or whether it bespeaks a refusal on the administration's part to honor and respect the constitutional limitations on its power is, I submit, quite irrelevant. The result is the same: interference with the rights of the faculty, and usurpation of power."

And then Oberhumer had rehashed eight or nine such "incidents": the downgrading of Education from a separate school to a department; the handling of the language requirements ("Hypocrite," Ritter said to himself, for Oberhumer had been the prime mover in abolishing Latin as a required subject); the restructuring of Economics; and several others. Each time he would add, "I don't question the decision itself, only the way in which the administration acted, the same way, pretty much, in which it has acted now in the Holloway matter in the Chemistry Department. I don't accuse the administration of intent to undermine the departmental chairs or to encroach on the autonomy of faculty. But that's the result. I don't consider this a matter of personalities. It's the absence of clear ground rules that makes for confusion."

Oberhumer was clever and effective, Ritter thought; but would he know when to stop? For his audience was becoming bored. Chairs began to scrape; there was coughing; in the back there was even some whispering; and Jerry Ashenbach was slumping back into near-somnolence. Oberhumer sensed this failing attention just in time. He stopped in mid-sentence and said: "All of us know that I could go on reciting similar incidents for a couple of hours—there have been far too many. I submit, Father Dean, that I have proven our need for constitutional clarification. I therefore move that the Academic Council adopt the following amendments to our by-laws: let me read them." And he whipped out a typewritten page while his sidekick Dr. Shoemacher, chairman of Life Sciences, produced a sheaf of copies and began to hand them out. Oberhumer read:

"(1) The Chairpersons of the all-university academic departments of St. Jerome University shall elect by secret ballot three of their colleagues to form an Executive Committee of the Faculty, each member to serve for three years and be eligible to be reelected once.

(2) In all matters affecting either curriculum or faculty, including appointment and termination, promotion, tenure, salary, and disciplinary action, the Executive Committee of the Faculty shall be the final decision-making organ of St. Jerome University, subject only to the powers of the Board of Regents. In particular, the Executive Committee of the Faculty shall be the only body empowered to make recommendations to the Board of Regents regarding faculty personnel, curriculum, and academic organization.

(3) Grievances, complaints, or disputes regarding promotion, tenure, teaching assignments, termination, or salary of a member of the faculty which cannot be settled within the appropriate academic department can be appealed only to the Executive Committee of the Faculty, whose decisions shall be considered final and binding.

"That," Oberhumer said softly, "should clarify matters." He sat down amid a stunned silence.

Ritter waited a minute, then asked dryly: "Anyone seconding?"

To everyone's surprise, including clearly Oberhumer's, it was not Dr. Shoemacher who first said: "I second the motion." It was a priest, Father Dennis Levecque, chairman of Economics.

Before Ritter could open the discussion, the dean of engineering was on his feet. "I have a question of clarification, Professor Oberhumer," he began. "As I read this, you propose to restrict administration to one main role: getting the money, with the faculty, or rather, the chairmen and chairwomen, deciding how and where to spend it, and how much. Am I right?"

"That's a pretty broad interpretation, Dean Grommet," Oberhumer responded, "a bit broader than I'd make it. But, yes, you're right, that's the general intention. I've never made any bones about my conviction that administration in a properly run university should be restricted to raising money, recruiting qualified students, and keeping house, and should leave all policy and personnel matters to the faculty."

After that it was a free-for-all. Ritter soon gave up keeping order or holding the discussion to any one topic. "Now I know," he said later to Bercovitz, describing the meeting, "how the Tower of Babel sounded. I've suffered through forty years of faculty meetings. But I've never sat through one as confused, undisciplined, or emotional as that, nor as nasty underneath."

"I told you, Father Dean, we are dealing with an attack of hysteria," was Bercovitz's only comment.

Very slowly the sense of the meeting began to swing against Oberhumer and his proposal. The chairmen and chairwomen were in a sullen mood all right; but they were not ready for revolution. "Another five minutes," Ritter said to himself, "and I'll call for the vote."

Then Father Boerhave, the chairman of Religion, who had so far stayed silent, bailed out Oberhumer—clearly without realizing what he was doing. "Father Dean," he said, "I believe that most of us would agree that we shouldn't vote on the spur of the moment on so difficult and serious a matter as constitutional reform. It deserves a lot of study and thought. I therefore hope that Professor Oberhumer will be willing to let me offer a substitute for his motion and withdraw his own for the time being. I would like to propose and to move: The Academic Council of St. Jerome University, conscious of the need to clarify the respective powers and responsibilities of administration and chairpersons in matters of faculty personnel and academic curriculum, and in order to clarify the relations between the two groups, hearby resolves that all communications to an individual faculty member from the university administration be henceforth channeled exclusively through the appropriate chairperson, and that no action with respect to an individual faculty member be taken by the administration either inside or outside the university except with the knowledge and concurrence of the appropriate academic chairperson.

"I submit, Father Dean," he added, "that this motion essentially represents the policy we thought we had all along. Apparently, it needs to be spelled out. And it does, I submit, accomplish Professor Oberhumer's main objective—to prevent what he calls 'incidents.' I only hope he'll be willing to withdraw his motion for the time being. We need to study it a little more carefully than we can in this meeting."

"Oh, sure," said Oberhumer, with a broad grin.

Five minutes later they voted. Boerhave's motion was roundly defeated—17 votes against 8 for, 7 abstentions. But it was a Pyrrhic victory for the administration. No sooner had Ritter announced the tally than Oberhumer got up and asked for a recount. Then he turned triumphantly to Ritter and said: "I hope you realize, Father Dean, that we only lost because of the votes of the eight deans. If you disregard their votes, and that of Dr. Ashenbach, who is also administration, and count only departmental chairpersons, that is, faculty, it's eight to eight with seven abstentions. And what may be more important in a Catholic university, out of the religious, the priests and nuns in departmental chairs, only one, Sister Malvina of Journalism, voted with the administration and against Father Boerhave's motion. One abstained, and six voted for the motion. That's hardly a resounding declaration of confidence in the administration by the university's faculty."

"I must correct you, Professor Oberhumer," said Erwin Ritter through clenched teeth. "Department chairpersons are as much 'administration' as a dean or the President. What's been defeated here today was an attempted power grab."

But Ritter knew that this was a half-truth. It was mutiny, and it had attained its main objective: to kick Heinz Zimmerman in the teeth.

Jerry Ashenbach, the physicist, and Dick Meyeroff, the Law School dean, walked together out of the meeting and down Campus Drive.

"What a disgusting farce," Meyeroff said bitterly. "I wonder how Erin Ritter kept his temper."

"Don't those idiots realize there'd *be* no St. Jerome without Zimmerman, no big jobs for them, no research grants or prestigious chairmanships," said Ashenbach, equally bitter. "I know what St. Jerome was like before Heinz took charge. I came here as an undergraduate on the G.I. Bill after World War II when the only decent job in the whole university was football coach. Of course, the lay faculty, some of them, at least, might have found good jobs elsewhere. But without Heinz Zimmerman, the St. Jerome priests would be teaching junior-high school with twenty-five hours of classroom work a week, instead of chairing a big, rich university department. And then they desert him at the very first vote and stab him in the back."

The two walked on in silence for five minutes until they came to the fork where one path led toward the Mulcahey Law Center and the other to the Advanced Physics Institute. There Ashenbach stopped again and said: "We've got to do something, and fast. I'm quite sure that no one, except Oberhumer perhaps, wants to see Zimmerman destroyed or damaged. But that's the way we're going. Maybe we ought to organize a meeting of senior faculty to affirm our support of Heinz, or get up a petition. It shouldn't be too difficult to get most of the senior faculty behind it."

"That's exactly what I've been thinking, Jerry," replied Meyeroff eagerly. "And you're right; it needs to be done swiftly. It shouldn't be too difficult. Let's you and me think about it for a day or two, then we'll decide what to do and do it fast."

And Meyeroff swung off toward his Law School with the stride of a man who has had a heavy burden lifted off his shoulders.

But in the end, neither Ashenbach nor Meyeroff would do anything.

Back at his office, Jerry Ashenbach tried to concentrate on the job he had been working on before he left for the Council meeting: the final proofs of a communication to *Physics Letters,* reporting important work done by one of his research fellows and himself. But his mind was still on Heinz Zimmerman.

"I'll finish the proofs at home," he said to his secretary, and left to talk to his wife, Gene.

It was because of Gene that the Ashenbachs were in Capital City. Gerhart Ashenbach, the son of a Capital City obstetrician, had become a full professor of physics at Princeton soon after he had published the Ashenbach equations for supercooled magnets, when not quite thirty. He would have been content to stay in Princeton the rest of his life. But Gene was becoming increasingly unhappy there. A first-rate viola player—she was the daughter of his boyhood cello teacher at Capital City—she felt frustrated by the lack of professional opportunities for a musician in Princeton, with both New York City and Philadelphia much too far for commuting.

He had mentioned this to Zimmerman when Heinz—his roommate in his freshman year at St. Jerome right after both had returned from wartime service—had come to stay with them in Princeton one weekend nine years ago. "That's wonderful," Heinz had said. "We can help each other, I'm sure. If I raise the money, would you be willing to move to St. Jerome and head a new Advanced Physics Institute? You'd have no teaching to do except what you yourself chose, enough money to bring in five or six outstanding young physicists as research fellows each year, and all the freedom you want for your own research and travel. And there's work aplenty in Capital City for a professional musician."

Less than a year later they had moved. It had worked out well for him—he actually got more work done than in Princeton where he had had a heavy load of doctoral students. And for Gene, Capital City was sheer bliss. She was the first viola on the Capital City Symphony, "one of the best American orchestras of the second rank, and on a par with Louisville, Kansas City, and Oklahoma," according to the music critic of the *New York Times,* and taught chamber music spring semesters at St. Mary in the Plains as her father had done before her.

Gene knew that she owed this happiness to Heinz Zimmerman. She would be outraged when he told her of the Council meeting. And with her quick, practical mind, she'd know right away what to do.

But to his surprise, Gene vetoed doing anything.

"Gerhart," she had protested immediately, "you must be out of your mind! You've practically got the Nobel Prize at last after being a finalist three times in a row. You know you should have gotten it years ago and would have if you'd stayed on at Princeton. But now that you've finally overcome the prejudice of those Swedes and the big-shot Eastern physicists against anything Catholic, you want to jeopardize it by taking the side of a 'reactionary' and opposing such 'liberal causes' as academic freedom and faculty autonomy. I could kick myself for letting you go to St. Jerome before you got the prize, but I didn't realize then how political this wretched Nobel business is. Now that it's within your reach again, I just won't let you throw it away!"

Dick Meyeroff, too, was stopped by his wife from taking any action on Heinz Zimmerman's behalf.

"No wonder you're upset," Sandra had said when he told her of the meeting. "I've known for a long time that academia is Peyton Place with Ph.D.'s. But this is going too far. I agree there's a need to do something. But you, Dick Meyeroff, are absolutely the last person to start it or even to take part in it. You stay out of it. That's an order, Counselor, not just a legal opinion.

"I know they're nice to you here, and Zimmerman and Ritter support you. But you're still an outsider—and a Jew. We Kesslers have been in this country and in Capital City for five generations, the Meyeroffs for only two. We've learned not to get in the middle when the Gentiles fight each other: they at once drop their fight and unite against the pushy Jew. And this is a fight among the priests. You have no more business taking part in it than a Nice Jewish Girl like me has in joining the Altar Guild. They'd cut you into little pieces and feed them to the ducks."

"I had no idea, Sandra," said Meyeroff, taken aback by her vehemence, "that you were so unhappy here."

"Oh you ninny," she cried, getting up from the sofa and coming over to his chair, where she sat on his lap and put her arms around his neck. "It's precisely because I *am* so happy here that I don't want you to do anything that would endanger us. I'm happy because you love the job and enjoy what you are doing. You'd never have gotten the opportunity any other place, surely not in Chicago, where a law school dean can only live up to a great past and mustn't make waves. And I'm back home where I grew up, in the city I love, where the Kesslers have been important for over a century as business leaders and pioneers. The children are happy here. They love going out to Grandfather's farm on weekends, riding the ponies and going fishing and being spoilt by our old servants. And soon I'll even be able to get a payoff from my law school degree— though I don't think I'll ever get a bigger payoff than I've gotten already: the handsomest law school prof as a husband and three lovely kids. But when Susan is in third grade I'll go to work as a lawyer in one of the family businesses, the insurance company maybe or the bank. Both Dannie and Bobbie want me.

"No, it's precisely because I'm so happy here that I don't want you to do anything to endanger our life. And believe me, if you get mixed up in that fight, whoever wins, you'll lose. Anyhow, why should *you* lead with your chin? What's Erwin Ritter doing?"

"What's Erwin Ritter doing?" Sandra Myeroff was not the only one asking the question. Even Ritter himself was asking it. And the answer was, As little as possible.

Not that he did not want to act—he itched for action. But whenever he felt like taking the initiative, Bercovitz dissuaded him:

"That's just what they want, Father Dean; hysterical people need publicity, they need to be taken seriously, they need to be important. The less attention you pay them, the sooner they'll tire of the game. Minimize it, don't play it up. As far as you're concerned, the faculty has reaffirmed what has been standard policy all along—that's how Father Boerhave introduced his resolution, isn't it? In due course, when the Regents meet here at the end of March, you'll report it to them with all the other unimportant resolutions the faculty has passed since the last Regents meeting before Christmas. You know how one treats a child in a tantrum, don't you? Well, hysteria is a grown-up tantrum."

It was not easy for Ritter to follow the advice. Things got rough right after the Council meeting and the silliest rumors began to sweep the campus. Suddenly there were stories that Heinz Zimmerman and Agnes Muller had been seen together coming out of, or checking into, a hotel in New York or Washington or Chicago. It was total fantasy, or course. Agnes Muller had never taken one day's vacation and always stayed behind to keep the office running when the president was away. But although this was common knowledge, it didn't seem to stop the rumors.

"Do you think, Dr. Bercovitz," Ritter asked, "that someone is deliberately plotting a smear campaign?"

"Possible, but unlikely," was the doctor's answer. "Anyone trying to spread poison deliberately would think up a better story. Such wild ones are precisely the ones hysteria breeds spontaneously."

But there were also rumors that the Regents had met in extraordinary and stormy session and had asked Heinz Zimmerman to resign; that he had refused, and that the Regents thereupon had secretly appointed a search committee to look for a successor.

Again, the story was patently absurd. There had been no Regents meeting at St. Jerome since before Christmas, well before the Holloway incident that had started all the trouble. And if there had been one off campus, neither Zimmerman nor Ritter could have attended since neither man had been away from St. Jerome for a single day in the last two months.

"Shall I point this out to a few of the senior faculty members, Dr. Bercovitz?" Ritter asked.

"I'd rather you didn't," was the answer. "Of course, you give them the facts should they ask. Otherwise you pretend you haven't heard anything deserving serious attention. And you haven't really, have you?"

Which was what Erwin Ritter then said to everybody who urged him to do something: to Dean Grommet of the Engineering School; to Father Hausman, dean of the undergraduate school of arts and sciences; to Ashenbach and Meyeroff; and to many others. Not everyone was happy with the answer, though Ashenbach and Meyeroff seemed relieved, Ritter thought; but they all accepted it.

Harder, much harder, to deal with were the "volunteers," as Bercovitz called them.

The first was Clement Boglund, chairman of Chemistry.

Boglund had begun to feel uneasy the moment Oberhumer started his speech. Although he had long come to understand why Zimmerman had been so gruff and upset when he called on him to talk about the Holloway phone call, Boglund still felt that he had been treated roughly. But Oberhumer, he thought, was turning a moment of rudeness into a court-martial offense. And as Oberhumer kept on talking, Boglund became progressively more wretched. Were Heinz Zimmerman and the university he had helped him to build going to be destroyed just because his, Boglund's, vanity had been piqued? Was he guilty of such gross self-indulgence, like a child spoilt rotten? If Oberhumer had gone on talking five minutes longer, Boglund would have voted against whatever motion he made or supported. He wavered, then caught Dennis Levecque's eye on him and abstained so as not to offend his closest friend.

But as soon as the vote was over, he began to curse himself for a fool and a coward. He spent a sleepless night becoming more and more upset by his own self-indulgence and irresponsibility. He had a class, his doctoral seminar, until eleven. Then he walked over to the Administration Building and into the dean's office and said:

"Erwin, I am here to offer my resignation as chairman of Chemistry and, if you think it'll help you or Heinz or St.

Jerome, my resignation from the faculty altogether. I have allowed pride and vanity to overrule my judgment and have made a mountain out of a trivial slight. And I've done what I cannot forgive myself for: I've harmed the university and you and Heinz Zimmerman, just because my feelings were hurt."

"You're dead wrong, and I won't let you resign," Ritter said immediately. "In the first place you had reason to be hurt. Heinz was thoughtless and impetuous. We both know he rarely is; but he was that morning. We know that it was a trying time for him and why; but that's an explanation, not an excuse. So forget it."

"But look at what Oberhumer did with it yesterday," protested Boglund.

"That's Oberhumer, not you. Anyhow, he'd have found something else to beat us with. You were simply the stick nearest to his hand. Not a very dignified role, I grant you, but hardly something to make speeches about."

But Boglund would not budge until Ritter had pointed out that his resigning would do real harm, indeed, far more harm than Oberhumer had been able to do so far.

"If you resign now, Clem," he had said, "everyone will be convinced that Zimmerman and I forced you to and did it to punish you. They'll be absolutely certain that you were fired. Then that little tiff you had with Heinz, the kind of thing that happens in a big organization every day, will assume monstrous proportions. You couldn't do anything that would help Oberhumer or discredit the administration and Heinz Zimmerman more. Don't you see that, Clem?"

The only thing Ritter achieved—and that took an hour's patient talking—was Boglund's promise to postpone any action until June and the end of the academic year.

"You'll have more 'volunteers,'" Bercovitz warned, when Ritter called him as soon as Boglund had left. "The belief in self-immolation to appease angry gods is strong in our hearts."

The next to offer herself up as a human sacrifice three days later was Agnes Muller.

*   *   *

"I have decided, Father Dean," she began, "that it is my duty to leave St. Jerome. It's the only home I have, and I've been happier here than I ever thought I could be. I don't know where I'm going to go or what I'm going to do the rest of my life. But I have no right to do more harm than I've already done. It was my selfishness that led to this vicious attack on Father President, which threatens his life's work. If I hadn't enjoyed working with him and serving him so much, I would have seen long ago that I was putting him in a false position and would have moved out of his office. I don't think he can ever trust me again."

She said all this with an appearance of utter calm and sweet reasonableness, as if she had carefully rehearsed it (as indeed she had). It was this rigid mask, this fiendish self-discipline, that infuriated Ritter. As he told Bercovitz later: "I felt like shaking her or choking her—anything to get her out of that martyr pose."

He didn't lay hands on her. But he did something as unprecedented, something no one in living memory had ever heard him do: he shouted at her so loudly that the secretaries in the adjoining offices came running out in near-panic:

"Stop feeling sorry for yourself, Agnes Muller, and wipe that self-righteous virgin smirk off your face! You aren't that important. So stop grandstanding."

Agnes's self-composure immediately crumpled. She began to sob wildly. "Father Dean," she said, when she could finally speak between her sobs. "I'm so ashamed. Not that people would say such things about me—I have been a married woman for a long time, after all, and have grown children. But that they can say such things about Father Heinz, and all because of me. And I'm afraid, too. Father Heinz is so changed. I hardly know him anymore. Oh, he's as polite and considerate to me as ever, and he lets me do even more of the work than before. But when he's alone and thinks himself unobserved, he just sits and stares into space or pretends to be busy without doing anything. He has to make a tremendous effort to be the Father Heinz we all know."

"Agnes," said Erwin Ritter, "that's more like you. Now you're making some sense.

"I sympathize with you; it must be very hard. But don't you see you mustn't desert Heinz now? Don't you see that now is the time when he needs everyone who loves him as you and I do? Forget that stupid rumor—you know that no one takes it seriously. You know how people love to gossip; it titillates. Is it the first time they've said things about you and another man? I bet is isn't. ("But I bet it is," said Erwin Ritter silently to himself). "Believe me, it isn't the first time they've said something about Father Heinz and women. That happens to every priest, and especially one like Heinz who takes his vows seriously. You'd only confirm the worst if you cut and run. It would be desertion in the face of the enemy.

"Yes, I realize Heinz is depressed," Ritter went on. "It's a rough time for him, and for all of us. But you know the university well enough to understand that the Holloway letter was only the match. Twenty years of rapid growth and success such as we've had create a lot of tension, a lot of friction. There are a number of people whose jobs have outgrown them and whose feelings of inadequacy make them bitter, suspicious, and hostile."

("I sound like Bercovitz," Erwin Ritter thought; and indeed he was repeating almost word for word arguments the psychiatrist had put forth just a day or two earlier. But they made sense to Agnes, who even raised a wan smile as if to say "I know exactly whom you have in mind.")

"Perhaps," Ritter continued, still paraphrasing Bercovitz, "it's a good thing that these tensions and problems are coming out, and that the occasion is nothing more serious than a poison-pen letter by a very sick woman. At least the boil is lanced.

"Believe me, Agnes, Heinz will bounce back. Just give him

a few weeks. Right now he needs you, he needs everyone who cares for him and believes in him."

All this took endless time. But in the end Agnes Muller had wiped the tears off her face, calmed down, promised not to do anything rash or foolish, and had left. But as she went out the door, Erwin Ritter for the first time noticed that she did not walk like a girl or a young woman; there was no spring to her step and no sway to her hips. For the first time she looked and moved middle-aged.

"But also," he said later to Bercovitz, "for the first time I really liked her."

It had taken Ritter many years to accept Agnes Muller. He could have accepted a nun. But a lay woman, in the inner circles of a university run by an Order of Brothers, and a married one to boot, he had found hard to swallow. Gradually, however, Agnes's performance, her quiet efficiency, her devotion to St. Jerome and to Heinz Zimmerman had won him over. Yet the very qualities he had come to admire in Agnes Muller, the assistant to the president, had made him feel quite uncomfortable about Agnes Muller, the woman.

"I'm an old existentialist," he told Bercovitz when he reported his conversation with Agnes. "I know that there is a dark, emotional side to us, a soul and passions and existential despair. And I had never even glimpsed those in Agnes; nothing but self-control, composure, evenness, rationality. I just didn't know or see anything but a mask. Now I feel I know a person and one, I am confident, I can trust."

In fact, Ritter had been badly shaken by Agnes's visit. As a teenager he had been feared for his violent outbursts; he had mastered his temper by the time he was twenty. But when Agnes Muller talked about quitting, a wave of rage rose up in him such as he had not known for more than forty years. It took all his strength to make himself keep his hands off her. He was still trembling when she left, ashamed of himself but also quite frightened. "So the distemper that's turning St. Jerome into a madhouse has gotten to me, too," he thought.

Even worse, he had lied to Agnes Muller, or, at least, he had withheld the truth. To be sure, what he had said about Zimmerman was exactly what Dr. Bercovitz had told him; and Bercovitz, the trained psychiatrist, was the expert in emotional problems, after all. But Ritter himself did not share the doctor's optimism, nor his certainty that Zimmerman would bounce back completely very soon. He could not figure out what ailed Heinz; but it was serious, and he was worried.

Erwin Ritter had always relied on prayer, and he prayed more and longer these days than he had ever done before. Yet when he got up from his knees, again and again he found himself quoting the despairing words of Claudius in *Hamlet*:

Words without thoughts never to heaven go.

He had the words. But he did not have the thoughts. He did not really know what he was praying for. He could not figure out what ailed Heinz Zimmerman.

"Have I pushed him too fast," Ritter asked himself; "have I made it so easy for him that he has no immunity at all, no antibodies against the common afflictions of life?" Bercovitz, to whom he submitted this question, thought it most unlikely. "After all, Heinz has had troubles and problems and fights enough in all these years. And many of them, I'd guess, were far more serious than this Holloway affair, which isn't even a tempest in a tea cup; more like a tempest in a demitasse. Have any of them ever bothered him before?"

Ritter had to admit that not one of them ever did. "On the contrary," he said, "every one brought out the *Raufhansl* in Heinz."

Now it was as if all the energy had been drained out of the man. When Ritter went past the president's office and looked through the open door, he saw Heinz sitting at his desk staring at his trophy wall. Later he asked Bercovitz, "Have you heard of *accidie?*" The doctor shook his head.

"It was the occupational disease of medieval monks," Ritter said. "The torpor of the soul from which few ever recovered. That's what Heinz's condition reminds me of. Is taking a part of his workload off his shoulders really the only thing I can do, doctor?"

"Yes," said Bercovitz. "A wound has to heal by itself."

But it was not the answer Ritter wanted to hear, and surely not enough help to give the man of whom his inner voice years ago had said, "This is your son."

"Can't I at least ask him what ails him, doctor?" he had persisted.

"That's the last thing you should do, Dean Ritter," Bercovitz replied firmly. "You must wait till he comes to you to talk."

But when Ritter one morning again passed by the president's office and saw Heinz sitting at his desk idly shuffling papers, he went in on impulse and asked: "What *is* the matter with you, Heinz? I can't understand you letting Oberhumer get under your skin like this."

"Oberhumer?" Zimmerman responded in a voice of amazement. "I don't even think of Oberhumer. Actually, Erwin"— and suddenly the old Heinz Zimmerman was back—"St. Jerome could do worse than elect Oberhumer President after I am gone."

"Are you joking, Heinz?" asked Ritter, quite startled.

"No, I'm not. Oberhumer is a great scholar with a worldwide reputation. He has standards. He has proven himself a first-rate administrator; look at the way he's built up his department in no time at all. He is excellent at raising money, better perhaps than I am. And no one else in the entire faculty really cares about the university and thinks about it. The others think only of their own fields and concerns."

"But what about all that drivel he's forever talking about, 'faculty democracy' and 'administrative tyranny'?"

Heinz Zimmerman chuckled. "I didn't think he'd take you in, Erwin. The day he becomes President, Oberhumer will forget every word he ever said on that subject, I guarantee you. Anyhow, he may have a point, you know. St. Jerome may be getting too big for the way you and I are running it. Our successors surely will have to manage it quite differently.

"All told, Erwin," Zimmerman continued, "it's not the faculty that's bothering me. Sure, it would be nice to get a little support. And it does hurt, I admit, that no one these last weeks has come forward to say 'Thank you' to you and me. But I didn't expect it. It's only a few weeks since you warned me, when you told me you want to step down as dean by the end of the year, that there really isn't anyone on the faculty who is committed head and heart to the first-rate Catholic university."

Zimmerman fell silent and began to play around with the papers on his desk. But just as Ritter thought he should get up and leave, he began again.

"What really bothers me," he said, "is that I can't figure out anymore why I am doing all this, and for whom. You know, Erwin, the inscription over the door to this building: *Ad majorem Dei gloriam?* Every morning when I come to work it's given me a lift all these years and made me say to myself: 'To the greater glory of God.'"

"Me, too," said Ritter.

"It doesn't any longer, not since this Holloway business started. It mocks me now, taunts me, says: *Ad majorem* Mei *gloriam.* It all seems nothing but vanity and personal ambition, aggrandizement and self-interest, and the desire to prove to myself that I'm a great man."

"Heinz," said Ritter, thoroughly alarmed, "stop at once. You're talking like a spoilt teenager. Have you forgotten all you ever learned in philosophy and logic and theology? Have you forgotten the definition of a saint as someone who knows where his true self-interest lies? That the work matters, and not the workman? Believe me, *not* to know what you've achieved would be worse than stupidity; it would be a sin."

"Erwin, I know you're trying to help and mean well," Zimmerman said with a wan smile. "I'm grateful, believe me. But what you're saying is pure sophistry, and you know it."

"I've been called worse names," Ritter responded, and there was suddenly deep anger beneath his bantering tone. "Being a sophist is, after all, part of a dean's job description. But, don't you see, you are letting all of us down—the Order and the university, me and all the faculty who look to you for leadership, and yourself worst of all. You can't just run away from responsibility to indulge yourself in hurt and self-pity."

But Heinz Zimmerman did not reply. He sat staring silently in front of him. When Ritter a few minutes later got up to leave, he nodded and let him go without another word.

Seymour Bercovitz also had a talk with Heinz Zimmerman.

It was after the weekly dinner at Bercovitz's place, when the two men sat down for their game of chess. They had already set up the board and chosen sides. Zimmerman had drawn white and the right to open; but instead of making the first move, he leaned back in his chair and said:

"Remember, Seymour, how you told me last fall why you dropped out of the seminary and didn't become a rabbi? I'd like to tell you now why I did become a priest.

"Of course, I'd given quite a bit of thought to my future career all those years in the army during World War II. But I knew then that I was much too fond of women to belong in the priesthood; I thought I'd probably become a teacher, though I had no idea of what. And then I came back to St. Jerome as a student on the G.I. Bill, determined to get a good education but also to have a good time after all those boring years in the service. I did well in my studies—it was easy enough. But that first year back at school I spent far more time sleeping around than with my books.

"And then I got a girl pregnant. She wanted to marry, of

course. But I didn't want to give up my freedom and I really didn't care that much for her, so I persuaded her to have an abortion. It wasn't easy then, you know. We neither of us had any money. And being Catholics—she was a sophomore at St. Mary in the Plains—we didn't know our way around and had no one we could ask for help. We finally found a woman who did abortions for the servant girls of Capital City. And she botched it. The girl got infected. She was in horrible pain and almost died. And all that week while I sat by her bedside in a mean little room downtown where the landlady extorted money from me with the threat of going to the police, I couldn't make myself even feel pity for that poor girl. All I could think about was that I would go to jail if she died. And then I realized that I hadn't ever cared for any of the girls I'd had affairs with, hadn't ever thought of them, but had just used them for my pleasure as if they were whores.

"As soon as that girl was out of danger and I had received absolution, I applied to become a priest.

"Why are you teling me all this, Heinz?" Bercovitz asked.

"Because I've realized in these last few weeks that I was quite mistaken about myself. I know now that I could have been as good a husband as any and as good a father."

"Do you regret that you went into the priesthood?"

"Oh, no, far from it. It was absolutely the right thing for me, absolutely my true vocation. Anything else would have been wrong for me. And that I did the right thing for the wrong reason, isn't that what we call Providence?

"You mean, Seymour, don't you, do I regret that I can't make love to Agnes and marry her? But it's a silly question. Agnes has made it clear, abundantly clear, that all she's interested in is her work and her working relationship with me.

"No, Seymour, what bothers me—upsets and confuses me—is that I realize I haven't changed. I am using people just exactly the way I used those girls before I went into the priesthood. Of course, I don't use them carnally. But I use them—and above all I use Agnes, for my purposes, to achieve what I want to achieve, and for my own satisfaction and self-glorification."

Long after Zimmerman had left, Bercovitz remained seated at the table looking at the chessboard. "Poor Heinz," he murmured to himself when, near midnight, he finally got up to put the set away. "He won't ever get back into the cocoon that has shielded him for thirty years. It'll be hard for him to have to learn to live with guilt and shame, self-doubt and ambiguity like all the rest of us."

PART FOUR

February turned into March—and early March was the meanest time of the year in Capital City, bringing the "Capital City specials": ice storms and freezing rains. Whoever could do so fled in early March. Jack Mulcahey, for instance, was in Palm Springs, and planning to stay there until the Regents' meeting at the end of the month. Phil Oberhumer, too, had escaped. He was in Ecuador or some such warm place on a geological survey for the World Bank.

What made early March particularly mean and depressing to the spirit were the first rare tantalizing glimpses of spring: a few days when the sky suddenly turned brilliantly blue, with small, fleecy white clouds sailing across it before a warm Southern breeze; when the first pussy willows were spotted on the banks of the still-frozen brook that meandered through the St. Jerome campus; and when a few hardy co-eds, like exotic butterflies, emerged from their winter cocoons of thermal underwear, longjohns, fur-lined boots and anoraks to sunbathe on the balconies of their dormitories in T-shirts and shorts. But these precious moments of spring were treacherous and deceptive. They actually signaled the next ice storm, or the next three-day freezing rain.

And yet—or so at least the optimists maintained—every one of these glimpses of spring lasted a little longer and every one brought a few more co-eds in T-shirts and shorts flaunting bare skin at the sun's rays and youthful laughter at middle-aged professors.

The emotional climate at St. Jerome that early March

faithfully mirrored the weather outside. It was very mean indeed.

Everybody knew, of course, that the story of an affair between Heinz Zimmerman and Agnes Muller was pure fabrication. But increasingly heads nodded when someone sagely observed: "Where there's smoke, there's fire." Ritter was tried almost beyond endurance when three of the elderly St. Jerome priests on the faculty—total nonentities each but old-timers still—cornered him after Sunday Mass one day and said: "We know there isn't anything to that story; it's a vicious lie. But the President of St. Jerome? Shouldn't he be like Caesar's wife and above suspicion? It surely can't be good for the university to have a President of whom such stories are being told, however unfounded."

When Ritter finished telling the three what he thought of them, they looked very small and apologized like children who know they have been naughty. But what those three had said to him, Ritter realized, others were saying among themselves, only knowing better than to mention it in his presence.

The faculty mutiny also had not come to an end with the Boerhave resolution, but smoldered on after the Council meeting. Twice within one week Oberhumer's sidekick, the Life Sciences chairman, stormed into Ritter's office to "lodge a formal protest" against some perfectly normal and harmless administrative action: first it was a circular letter to all faculty members on the tenure track, advising them of the changes in tenure policy the Council had voted on; then it was a letter to all faculty reminding them that the dean's office had to sanction the use of a nonfaculty member as a substitute instructor for an absent professor. "I know that the Boerhave resolution didn't pass," Dr. Shoemacher said glibly. "But it was defeated because we were assured that it only codified already existing policy and was redundant. And now you are violating it both in letter and in spirit. Clearly, the administration has no intention of respecting the rights of chairpersons or of the faculty altogether, no intention of playing by the rules it officially endorses. We'll have something to say about this at the next Council meeting; and Phil Oberhumer will be back then."

What made this a genuine threat was that the Life Sciences chairman both times was accompanied by Dennis Levecque of Economics. Apparently the unholy alliance between "Great Research University" and "Great Catholic University"—the alliance to tear down Heinz Zimmerman and the university's administration—still held together.

Then, just like the weather outside, March began to bring the first signs of spring to the emotional climate. Or, rather, there were signs of a return to more normal, more conventional, more traditional turbulences. And as in the weather outside, the optimists could discern in the emotional climate that these intervals of normality were becoming more frequent and were lasting longer, and that they increasingly diverted the faculty from Heinz Zimmerman and the "Holloway Affair"—as it was now called by everyone, including the majority who had no idea who or what Holloway was—to more normal follies and idiocies, and especially to the deeply cherished traditional feuds of academia.

First there came an outbreak of the perennial wrangle between chairpersons of the university-wide departments and the deans of the individual schools over the assignment of teaching faculty. Did the schools, Business, say, or Engineering, have a veto power over which English or Physics instructor was assigned to teach in them? Was it perhaps even *their* job to decide which instructor should teach their students? Or did this power rest with the department and its chairperson?

Normally these silly disputes both disgusted and bored Erwin Ritter, and he settled them by banging heads together. They annoyed him just as much this March, but he almost welcomed them as the first sign that St. Jerome was moving back from a singularly mean to a normally silly season.

And then, right on schedule in the second week of March arrived the Annual Athletic Feud. In the twenty-seven years during which Ritter had been dean, there had been six or seven different athletic directors at St. Jerome. And each, the second week of March, had called a press conference of the state's sportswriters and started a public, raucous fight with one of the coaches. It would have been as funny as a Punch and Judy show if it had not been so drearily vulgar.

This year, Father Bernardi, the athletic director and the only St. Jerome football player ever to make All-American, called for the dismissal of the football coach, who had just concluded his fourth victorious season and was the hero of students and alumni alike. "He pads his expense account," he proclaimed; "and what's worse, his entertainment charges are not for high-school football coaches and prospective players. His guests are all female!"

Students took sides with gusto, and so did alumni. During one morning Erwin Ritter answered twenty-four phone calls from alumni, half demanding the coach's immediate discharge, the other half threatening to cancel their annual donation unless the athletic director was fired. But football was important also to the faculty, and especially to the priests on the faculty. In a stormy meeting in Ritter's office, Father Carstens, the senior priest on the faculty, chairman of Religion and of the Faculty Athletics Committee, and a football fan, screamed at Father Bernardi: "The coach is a layman and you have no goddamn business poking into his sex life!"

"I don't give a shit for his sex life," Bernardi screamed back; "he's a crook and steals from the university!"

Ritter had always dreaded the Annual Athletic Feud. But this year he reveled in it, even mischievously encouraged it. It was a nagging toothache; but at least it wasn't cancer.

And then at last Heinz Zimmerman was beginning to have sunny intervals, though for most of the time he was still as unfriendly, as gray and cloud-shrouded, as the March sky.

The first Sunday in March, Heinz even accepted an invitation, tendered him at Ritter's insistence, to have lunch with

Erwin at Agnes Muller's house. As Agnes had predicted, her food was infinitely better than what the lay brothers provided at the president's residence, and all three greatly enjoyed the meal.

In the office, too, the old harmony seemed to reestablish itself. An extra desk still stood in Agnes's office. But it was unoccupied, Mrs. Lopez long ago having fled to the cozier atmosphere of the typists' pool with its coffee breaks and its companionable chats. Heinz Zimmerman and Agnes Muller were back at their old routine and the door between their offices was kept open again. If there was a change, it was that the president delegated far more to Agnes than he had ever done before and kept her working until late at night most days. But she didn't complain; at least Heinz hadn't lost his trust in her.

When the check for the first installment on the oil millionaire's pledge came in, Zimmerman threw a victory party in his office for his entire Executive Committee. And to everyone's surprise he proposed a formal vote of thanks to Philip Oberhumer, "who has done so much to bring to St. Jerome first-rate science and the means to sustain it."

In mid-March, almost five weeks after the Holloways had called on him that disastrous Sunday afternoon, the old Heinz Zimmerman, the forceful executive, finally reappeared, if only for an instant. All deans and chairpersons found in their mail a Letter from the President, which read:

As you probably know, we intend to introduce during the next two academic years, that is between now and Spring Semester 1982, a required non-credit computer course in all professional schools— similar to the one already being taught in the Engineering and Management Schools. Within another twelve months we should then begin to introduce the same required non-credit course for undergraduates majoring in a science or social science or enrolled in the premedical program. We ourselves therefore had better make sure that we know what the computer is all about. I have arranged for computer courses for deans and chairpersons to be given on six

consecutive Saturday evenings, the first to start on April 15. I myself have enrolled—please let me know when you intend to take it.

Erwin Ritter had tears in his eyes as he phoned Dr. Bercovitz to read him the letter. "Yes," said Seymour (they were
beginning to be on a first-name basis), "that's the light at the
end of the tunnel. I am a little bit superstitious. Accidents do
happen, so I don't want to shout 'Hallelujah' yet. But barring
an accident, this nasty affair should be behind us by the time
your Regents meet for their next session at the end of the
month. And then I'll invite you and Heinz and Agnes Muller
to the best dinner I can serve—I'll cook and you can bring the
champagne."

The Voice of Reason had had substantial circulation and
considerable influence in the twenties, and even more so in
the thirties when, faithfully following every twist and turn in
the Stalinist line and nicknamed *The Voice of Treason*, it had
been the house organ of fellow travelers in academia, journalism, and Hollywood.

It had died long before 1980, however. And the only reason
the corpse had not been buried was that the founder, heiress
to a Chicago meat-packing fortune, had made all the pay-
ments from her estate to her only son dependent on his continuing weekly publication of the magazine. Circulation had
shrunk to 8,000, most of which went to libraries where no one
read the copies. Advertising had disappeared except for a few
pathetic "Personals": "Intelligent woman, college degree, still
young, seeks correspondence with mature male professional
who shares her interests in chamber music and progressive
causes." And the magazine itself, both in its Art Nouveau
layout and in the references to Sacco and Vanzetti and the
Scottsboro Boys that studded its editorial pages, looked and
smelled as musty as a bachelor's laundry hamper left unemp-
tied the entire summer.

As far as anyone could discover, *The Voice of Reason* had

only one subscriber in Capital City: the library of St. Jerome University. The librarian there had already decided not to renew; for quite a few years now she had not seen anybody take it up from the shelves, let alone read it. But within two days after she put the newly arrived issue, dated March 22, 1980, in the Periodicals Room, every one of the 970 members of the St. Jerome faculty, down to the lowliest graduate assistant, had seen and read a copy of the editorial that was advertised on the magazine's bright red cover in big black letters:

EDITORIAL: THE CASE OF ST. JEROME U.

When several months ago we discussed the remarkable address on the "Great Catholic University" by Heinz Zimmerman, monk and president of a Catholic university calling itself St. Jerome University, we were sharply criticized. We had pointed out the incompatibility of the beliefs and practices of the Roman Church: the Inquisition; the Index of Forbidden Books; Papal Infallibility; and the Roman Church's claim to have the duty to control the minds, morals, and beliefs of its members, with the very values—freedom of inquiry, thought, and expression, and the supremacy of reason as against revelation and dogma—on which any institution deserving the name "university" must be based.

This, we were told by several correspondents, is anachronistic. Today's Catholic Church, they asserted, has changed its spots. It has embraced the beliefs of an open democratic society. Some of the letters even called us "old-fashioned" and "bigoted."

Now hear this! A most distinguished scientist on the St. Jerome University faculty, a geologist of world renown, felt it necessary recently to put forth a motion of censure against the apostle of the "Great Catholic University," Heinz Zimmerman, monk and president, for grossly violating the rights of the faculty and interfering willfully with faculty autonomy. When it came to the vote, only eight of the twenty-three departmental chairpersons—a bare one third—sided with the president and the university's administration over this issue. The majority even of the Catholic monks and priests in departmental chairs did not support the president in this vote, which surely argues that there is not, at St. Jerome University, enough respect for faculty rights and faculty autonomy to satisfy even the (presumably fairly modest) expectations of monks and nuns as to what a "university" has to be. And not one of the distinguished scholars and scientists whom Dr. Zimmerman has recruited for the faculty of St. Jerome University has seen fit since to speak out in defense of the university's administration.

We are further informed that there is a move afoot, especially among the monks and priests, to oust Dr. Zimmerman as president of St. Jerome University because of an alleged romantic involvement with a lady on his staff—both of them adults, of course, and, incidentally, unmarried. To consider the private life and behavior of a member of the academic community a public concern and relevant to the individual's fitness for office is as incompatible with what a "university" is all about as is thought control and administrative interference with faculty autonomy and academic freedom. Yet it is inherent in the creed, laws, and practices of the Roman Church.

Can there really be a "Catholic University," let alone a "Great Catholic University"? Has the Roman Church changed its spots—or is it still the Church of the Inquisition, of the Index of Forbidden Books, of Papal Infallibility, and of obscurantism and thought control?

And who deserves to be called "bigoted"?

"The Great Stone Face," Heinz Zimmerman had once, at a staff party, called Dean Ritter's long-time secretary; she had been so pleased with the compliment that she almost smiled. But when she brought back a Xerox copy of the editorial from her morning coffee break, "The Great Stone Face" was so upset that her voice broke. Her hands shook violently as she thrust the sheet across his desk at her boss.

"You ought to know by now," Ritter said mildly after he had read the page slowly twice, "that some people don't much like Catholics. Otherwise I see nothing in here that deserves getting excited about."

But few members of the faculty shared Erwin Ritter's opinion. No event in the whole history of St. Jerome—not even the merger with a woman's college, St. Mary in the Plains, which the priests on the faculty and the alumni had fought bitterly for three long years—had ever set off a firestorm comparable to the one unleashed by *The Voice of Reason*.

Ten or fifteen minutes after Ritter had read the editorial, Dennis Levecque burst into his office waving a copy of the sheet, almost blue in the face with rage and shouting at the top of his lungs: "Erwin, we'll sue the bastards for libel and get the last penny in damages out of them. This is an outrage!"

"Now wait a minute, Dennis," Ritter said with a touch of self-righteousness in his voice. "Of course the piece distorts. But everything it says is factual. What did you think Oberhumer's motion was if not a declaration of nonconfidence in Heinz Zimmerman and the St. Jerome administration? And who was the first to second it? You, Dennis."

"But you know, and so did everybody else in the meeting, that that wasn't my intention. You know I'd never attack St. Jerome."

"That time you did, Dennis," said Ritter dryly. "How do you think you'd look on the witness stand admitting that you immediately seconded the Oberhumer motion, but claiming that you never intended to do what you did?"

Dennis Levecque would not abandon his demand that St. Jerome should sue *The Voice of Reason* for libel, or, he said, "for defamation of character or invasion of privacy or slander or whatever else the lawyers can think up," until both Sister Renée, the public-relations vice president, and the university's outside lawyers had confirmed that there were no possible grounds for a suit. Even then, he wanted the university to demand a public retraction; and he actually drafted a Letter to the Editor protesting that he had never meant what the editorial imputed to him.

When Levecque finally had to admit that ignoring the editorial was the only possible course, he turned on Ritter: "Why didn't you warn me, Erwin, that I would be totally misunderstood? You saw it, yet you didn't do anything to stop me or protect me. You and Heinz Zimmerman let me down. I'll never forgive the two of you!"

No sooner had Erwin Ritter disposed of Levecque than he had to deal with Jim Schenk, a professor of classics and one of the oldest of the St. Jerome priests on the faculty. It was Schenk whom Ritter had taken to task a few days earlier for worrying about the damage which the rumor of an affair between Heinz Zimmerman and Agnes Muller might do to the university and the Order. "Now you see, Erwin," Jim Schenk said, "that we were right to worry. Zimmerman is endangering St. Jerome and all of us by his imprudence. The sooner he quits as President, the sooner this will be forgotten."

"You know there's nothing to the story, don't you, Jim?" Ritter asked. Father Schenk nodded. "Now, how would you feel if there were such a story about you, which all of us knew to be totally groundless and pure fabrication, and we asked you to resign?"

"But, Erwin," Schenk retorted, "I'm a nobody, not the university's President, a national figure and on the cover of *Time*. What I do and what they say about me cannot possibly harm anyone but myself. But a man in Zimmerman's position has failed in his duty if he gets attacked like this, even if it's totally groundless. He has given aid and comfort to the enemy"—and Schenk rambled off into a long quotation from Horace or Virgil.

Then there were the deans and chairpersons and professors who earlier had wanted "to do something" or had wanted Ritter "to do something." Each of them now came and blamed Ritter for putting them in a position where *The Voice of Reason* could point to their inaction as proof of their joining in the attack on Zimmerman. Even Zimmerman himself, showing normal emotions for the first time in weeks, came to Ritter to complain about being attacked and vilified and wanting to know what the university could and should do about it.

And Agnes Muller came back to offer her resignation once more and to blame herself again for having betrayed Heinz

Zimmerman and St. Jerome. "At least," thought Ritter, "she blames herself. All the others blame Zimmerman or me."

But whereas St. Jerome was erupting like a volcanic park with geysers and foul-smelling gases, mudslides and minor earthquakes, no one on the outside, it seemed, paid the slightest attention to *The Voice of Reason* and its editorial. Apparently nobody had seen the piece, let alone read it.

"You insult me, Sister Renée," the editor of the *Capital City Gazette*, the state's leading morning paper, said when she called him to make sure he wouldn't run the story. "I'd be ashamed to take note of anything that appears in that rag."

The much younger editor of the smaller but friskier afternoon paper, the *News* (a newcomer to Capital City, where he had moved only three years earlier) had never even heard of *The Voice of Reason*. "Sounds like something that was published during the American Revolution," he said. "Hold on, that was *The Age of Reason*, wasn't it?" And when he was read the editorial over the phone, he chortled and said: "Sister Renée, any news about St. Jerome University is news in Capital City. But don't tell me this is *news*. Maybe the fact that a faculty and its president *aren't* squabbling might be news these days. But who cares for faculty motions? And even though I'm a practicing Catholic myself, I couldn't get excited these days about a story of a priest having a girl friend, whether it's true or not."

Nor did Seymour Bercovitz seem perturbed when Ritter phoned him. "What," he said, "*The Voice of Reason* still exists? My father used to subscribe to it some forty years ago when I was a youngster. He dropped his subscription when it endorsed the Stalin-Hitler Pact in 1939. Since then I haven't even heard of the sheet—and I daresay nobody else has, either. No one reads it. No one pays any attention to it. I bet you nobody under fifty today has even heard of it. You wouldn't pay much attention to a story about St. Jerome in the *Arkansas Beekeeper* or the *Idaho Turnip Grower*, would you? Then why pay attention to *The Voice of Reason*?"

Which was what Erwin Ritter then told everyone on his own faculty, as well as Heinz Zimmerman and Agnes Muller.

"No one reads the sheet or even knows about it," Ritter also said to Father Tom Martini, when the young priest called to enquire what he should tell his bishop.

Martini himself had never heard of *The Voice of Reason*. But when one of the young priests on the St. Jerome faculty— a former classmate in the seminary—told him of the editorial, he thought it his duty to show it to Bishop O'Malley; after all, St. Jerome was in the bishop's diocese. He could not, however, find a single copy anywhere in Capital City. The magazine was not in the public library nor in the state house nor in the legislative reference library of the state legislature. Indeed, the three librarians of these institutions assured him that it had long ceased to exist. He had to drive out to St. Jerome and its library to find a copy to Xerox, and then called on Dean Ritter to find out what he should tell Bishop O'Malley and, indeed, what all the fuss was about.

And so when, the following morning, Monsignor Allesandri called from Washington and asked the bishop about the editorial, O'Malley answered: "Pay no attention; I myself didn't know that this magazine is still being published. And as far as we can figure out, there is just one subscriber in all of Capital City, the St. Jerome University Library. Nobody reads the sheet."

"I don't think, Patrick," said Allessandri in the bantering tone which he only used when he was in deadly earnest, "you'd call His Excellency the Nuncio a 'nobody.' He has read the editorial and is quite perturbed by it.

"But that's not the main reason why I'm calling. Patrick, Rome wants to know about this editorial and what's going on at St. Jerome. You may be right about the unimportance of *The Voice of Reason* in the United States. I admit I myself had never heard of the magazine. But in Italy and Spain and Portugal, and especially in the Soviet bloc countries with large Catholic populations—Hungary, Poland, Czechoslovakia, and East Germany—*The Voice of Reason* is still widely quoted and considered the liberal conscience of the United States, its one 'progressive' publication and the true voice of the repressed proletarian masses of America. This editorial is bound to be picked up and reprinted widely; it's just too convenient for those, in Poland, for instance, who want to discredit the Church's demand for a bigger say in higher education. Of course it won't matter if that happens in the daily press. But if the intellectual monthlies of the left in France or Italy run with it, it could do a good deal of damage—and it couldn't come at a worse time than now when Rome, for the first time, sees a chance for a dialogue with the intellectuals on the left."

Monsignor Allessandri paused ("He's consulting his notes," Bishop O'Malley thought), then continued in a brisker tone. "I would have called you up anyhow, Patrick, to give you good news. Your request to Rome to raise Capital City to an archbishopric is doing much better than I dared hope. You were right: Rome has wanted to do this all along and was just waiting for the proper moment.

"But if you don't do something to show that there is no substance whatever to this attack on a leading Catholic university and a prominent American priest—both in your diocese—well, Patrick, you know how timid the Curia is.

"I'll tell His Excellency the Nuncio what you've told me about *The Voice of Reason*, and I'll pass it on to Rome, of course. But, Patrick, what is the name of that brilliant young diplomat, your secretary?—ah yes, Father Tom Martini—one of your good Irish names, I take it. Why don't you put this young man on the job to extricate yourself and this Father Heinz Zimmerman, and to find a solution that shows this attack is a lie and there's no scandal brewing at St. Jerome University, and no unseemly quarrel among the priests in your diocese?"

*   *   *

"I don't really know how to explain it," a deeply disturbed Tom Martini said three days later to his Bishop. "There's something terribly wrong at St. Jerome. But I can't figure out what it is. The little that's tangible is all trivia. I was reminded the whole time of when I was twelve or thirteen and my sister and I used to bitch and scream at each other: 'You've used my scissors without asking my permission!' It's all on that level. It's one man's wounded ego and another man's envy and gossip and backbiting. But it's sick, very sick. Dean Ritter holds the place together, sort of; but he's hanging on for dear life and doesn't seem to know what to do, or even whether to do anything. Yet the place is losing its self-confidence and decency and cohesion by the hour.

"Everyone blames somebody else for starting the trouble. The priests blame the lay faculty, and both blame the Order's General or the chairman of the Regents. And everyone protests that he himself, of course, is totally blameless and has done nothing but pour oil on troubled waters."

"'And Brutus is an honorable man,'" Bishop O'Malley said, half under his breath.

"And the worst of it," Tom Martini continued, "is that every one of these great scholars and good Christians blames Father Zimmerman. And when you ask them what Father Zimmerman has done to be blamed for, they say in effect: 'He hasn't done anything but shouldn't have done it.' I felt like throwing up the whole time I was out there.

"And yet," added Martini after a short pause, "I just can't figure out what all this nastiness is about. The only specific complaint—if you can call it that—is that Father Zimmerman disregarded etiquette and phoned directly to a neighboring women's college to find a job for a middle-aged professor whose contract won't be renewed, instead of going through the department chairman. Everyone admits he did it out of pity for the man, but says he shouldn't have done it."

"'And Brutus is an honorable man,'" the bishop muttered again.

"But the worst of it, sir," Martini went on, "is Father Zimmerman's having given up. He's a defeated man, and no one can figure out why. He sits in his office, leaving everything to Dean Ritter; he hardly speaks to people.

"Dean Ritter asked me to have a word with a friend of his and of Father Zimmerman's, a Dr. Bercovitz, a psychiatrist. He's the State Commissioner of Mental Health. Do you know of him, sir?"

"I've heard he's a competent man," the bishop answered. "What did he tell you?"

"He called the Holloway Affair a 'storm in a demitasse'— rather clever, I thought, and quite apt. Of course, he's right. It's a petty business. But to use his metaphor, it's cracked the demitasse to where it can't be glued together again. I don't see how Father Zimmerman can ever again truly run the place the way he used to and the way it should be run. Not because St. Jerome won't accept his leadership. I agree with Dean Ritter that it wouldn't take much to get the St. Jerome faculty to return to sanity and self-discipline, if only Father Zimmerman took the lead and asserted himself. The faculty itself, I'd say, is quite scared of the mischief it's been making. But I don't see Father Zimmerman recovering. Whatever ails him, he seems to have lost his self-confidence and his belief in himself and what he's been doing. He hasn't been dethroned; he abdicated at the first challenge."

"All these trivia you describe," said the bishop thoughtfully, "are just symptoms, I'd say. The real issues, I am convinced, go much deeper. Twenty years of mushroom growth has pushed everything out of alignment at the university, so that no one can really know what the rules are. Worse, there is still the unanswerable question of what a Catholic university has to do in order to be first-rate, or a 'first-rate university' has to do to be Catholic—you remember our talk a few weeks back?

"But, Tom, no matter what the real issues are, we have to help Heinz Zimmerman. His only offense is in having yielded to the temptation to do good and behave like a Christian and a priest rather than a bureaucrat."

"I don't know, sir," Martini replied, "what we could do. The place is so totally demoralized. Do you remember Hemingway's *Farewell to Arms*?"

The bishop nodded.

"The rout of the Italian Army after the Austrians smashed it in World War I? I read that chapter over again last night to make sure I remembered it right. That's what St. Jerome reminds me of: a lot of defeated and leaderless people running away in all directions, united only in their hatred of their own High Command."

"And do *you* know, Tom," the bishop said with sudden animation, "what stopped that rout of the Italian Army after Caporetto? Of course you don't; I don't think it's in the novel. What made the Italians become an army again were the big naval guns of the English and French fleets in the Mediterranean. They were hauled on land and began to bombard the retreating Italians, who were left no choice but to turn around and fight the enemy again.

"Well, in the Church, the bishop is the big gun. It's my job to stop this poisonous rot at St. Jerome. After all, this is *my* diocese, not the diocese of the Nuncio or Monsignor Allessandri. And the priests at St. Jerome are priests in *my* diocese. I am responsible for their behavior. I don't know precisely yet what I'll do. But at the very least I'll call in the St. Jerome priests one by one, read them the riot act, and threaten them with everything I can think of unless they rally behind Heinz Zimmerman. I'll be the naval gun; I'll make such a noise that they'll have to listen!

"I know, Tom, you'll remind me that I'm critical of Father Zimmerman and very dubious about his whole policy. But that's got nothing to do with it; it's a matter of common decency and conscience. What's going to happen later at St. Jerome, we'll see. But first it's my duty to protect Heinz Zimmerman."

"The Nuncio and Monsignor Allessandri will hardly like this," the startled Tom Martini said. "What will it do to your request to have Capital City raised to an archbishopric?"

"The good Catholic people of Capital City," the bishop said with something like a smile in his voice, "will just have to survive without it for another ten or twenty years. The Nuncio might not get to be proto-Secretary of State and a cardinal when he returns to Rome in a few years. And Allessandri might have to wait a mite longer for the bishopric he wants so badly he can taste it." ("And you, Tom," the bishop added to himself, "might end up a vice chancellor rather than a bishop.") "But I haven't taken an oath to further the Nuncio's career. My duty is to this diocese."

"You make it sound very grim, Bishop," Tom Martini said. "Don't you see any way out?"

"There's always one," the bishop said. "It's called a miracle. Sure, I'd rather not have to wade into this sewer and play the heavy, and no one is going to thank me for it either, least of all Zimmerman. It would be nice if the Lord sent down a fiery chariot for Heinz. But miracles, Tom, don't happen just because you and I want to avoid unpleasantness.

"No, we'll have to fight this one out—never mind *The Voice of Reason* and Rome and the Nuncio and Monsignor Allessandri. Why don't you go downstairs and huddle with Bernie Murtagh and work out a plan of action—no one around here knows politics as well as Bernie. And then I'll go to work. I don't think we can wait for Providence to do the job for us."

But Providence did in fact intervene, although Bishop O'Malley was to wonder more than once whether the miracle had been sent from above or from below.

Bernie Murtagh was on the telephone when Tom Martini entered his office. He was talking in the exaggerated Irish brogue—a vaudeville actor of the twenties would have been ashamed to affect it—he only used when speaking to politicians. But he cupped a hand over the receiver and muttered, "Won't be a minute," while waving Martini to a chair.

"Faith, Timmy-me-lad," he said heartily into the phone, "you're in a fine pickle. But we'll find a solution, trust me. Give me a while to think and I'll be back at you."

"Quite unimportant and can wait," he said in his usual voice when he had hung up. "Now, what can I do for His Efficiency?"

"You know anything about the troubles at St. Jerome University, Bernie?" Martini began. And when Murtagh shook his head, Tom started to tell him the story. At first Murtagh listened in silence. Then he began to ask questions, got Tom to repeat parts of the story, wanted more details, and became more and more interested. And when Tom finally got to telling him what the bishop had said about "a miracle," Bernie Murtagh burst into loud laughter. "So, His Efficiency doesn't believe in miracles! Maybe what we have won't quite satisfy the canon lawyers and the theologians, they're so picky. But it's miracle enough for me."

Martini stared at him with wide-open eyes.

"I was talking to Timothy Doyle when you came in, Tom," Murtagh said. "The name mean anything to you?"

Martini shook his head.

"Officially he is State Highway Commissioner. He's Governor Ewing's political adviser and his campaign manager.

"You know anything about the politics in this state, Tom, or do you only read the *Diocesan Messenger*? Okay, let me brief you. You know this is normally a Republican state?" Martini nodded. "And you do know that three and a half years ago we elected a Democrat as Governor in the backlash against Watergate, for the first time since New Deal days and with a greater majority than the one with which Jimmy Carter carried the state? And I imagine you know that Governor Ewing comes up for reelection this fall, and that the state is rapidly moving back into the Republican column, even though Ewing himself is remarkably popular?"

Martini nodded a few more times.

"But I bet you, Tom," Murtagh continued, "that you do not know that our last Republican governor, Colebrooke, who will try for a comeback this fall, created a Civil Rights Commission in a bid for the votes of the liberals and the minorities and especially the blacks the year before he was defeated for reelection? You ever heard of it?" Martini shook his head.

"You and the other seven million citizens of this great state," commented Murtagh.

"I bet you also never heard of the Reverend Thomas Langley Gould of the African Methodist Church? No, you're too young. Fifteen, twenty years ago he cut quite a figure in the state—a friend of Dr. Martin Luther King, a participant in the March on Selma, prominent black orator, invited by the Kennedys to the White House, and so on. A pompous windbag, actually, and he never did anything but chase publicity. Governor Colebrooke made him chairman of the Civil Rights Commission and its one and only full-time paid commissioner with a fat salary and a big staff. Of course, you don't know any of this—you weren't meant to. For Gould wasn't appointed to *do* anything. His appointment was intended to satisfy the blacks without upsetting anyone else. And everybody was perfectly happy to have him do nothing except make a few speeches and travel the state accompanied by three or four very young, very lush secretaries."

"You're a cynic, Bernie," Martini said.

"No, Tom, I am not, otherwise I'd have gone into real estate rather than politics.

"But let me go on with what Tim Doyle was telling me when you just came in. Everything was hunky-dory. The governor was going to reappoint the Reverend Thomas Langley Gould to another five-year term as chairman at $62,500 a year when his appointment expires next month—I think Doyle said the date is April 15. Then, to use Doyle's words: 'The bastard double-crossed the governor and suddenly died,' three weeks ago. And now the governor is on the hook. What should have been routine has become a life-and-death matter. There are more than enough candidates for the job. But to appoint any one of them would cost our governor the election sure as God made little apples.

"The blacks want one of their own again, of course. And they do have a candidate: Ralph Christenberry of the state AFL-CIO."

"Oh no," said Martini.

"Oh yes," said Murtagh. "I see you *do* read something beside the *Diocesan Messenger*, so you know that Christenberry as AFL-CIO state director made headlines a few months ago by coming out for the PLO and against Israel, and by that violent attack on the Jews in which he called them 'Sheenies,' 'Shylocks,' and 'Yids.' I don't have to tell you what the reaction of the liberals and the Jewish business community would be to having *him* appointed chairman of the Civil Rights Commission. The governor desperately needs the campaign contributions from the Jewish business community, the Fynemans and Kesslers and the rest of them.

"But what you can't know, Tom—unless you also read *La Causa*, the Spanish-language weekly—is that Mr. Christenberry also attacked the Chicanos in the state, accusing them of taking jobs away from decent American workers and demanding an end to immigration from Mexico and deportation of all illegal Mexican aliens. I don't know what Christenberry's game is. I suspect he plans to run for Congress from the solidly black district on the south side of town. But in any event he can't be appointed—and yet he refuses to withdraw, and the blacks refuse to nominate another black for the job.

"The Hispanics have nominated a Professor Fernandez— he teaches at one of the state colleges—who has come out against busing and accused the state government of favoring blacks over Hispanics. And the liberals have a candidate of their own, supported by the business community. He's Judge Rosenbaum, of the State Court of Appeals, who was chairman of Americans for Democratic Action in the state and is married to one of the department-store Fynemans.

"Do you see now why your Father Zimmerman is a miracle? He'll get everybody off the hook—not just you and the bishop and St. Jerome but the governor and everyone else. You tell me he was on President Johnson's Civil Rights Commission? Wonderful. We have a thirty percent Catholic population in this state. He's a distinguished educator and he's never before taken part in local politics and has no enemies. He couldn't be better!

"Let me just check back with Tim Doyle. Of course I'll tell him it would be a miracle if Father Zimmerman were willing to accept the job. And then let's go to work—we have very little time."

Tom Martini could never remember much of the next few days. They were a blur of endless telephone calls, meetings at odd hours, hasty conferences, and improbable "crises." He could not recall having gone to bed at all during those days, nor having eaten. Most of the time, it seemed to him, was spent sitting in Sister Renée's conference room (it had become their command post) and waiting, waiting, waiting.

"I don't think we can get the ideal," she warned, "a public offer of the job to Father Zimmerman, which he could then turn down but which would show everyone inside and outside the university that there's nothing to these vicious rumors. Tim Doyle is too shrewd to go out on that limb. But if we get an offer at all—and I think we have a chance—and Father Zimmerman can be persuaded to take it, I'd say a hundred Hail Marys."

Sister Renée immediately mobilized her contacts in the state government, the governor's press secretary and the social secretary of the governor's wife, both alumnae of St. Mary in the Plains and both enthusiastically willing to help. She also dispatched Tom Martini to enlist Seymour Bercovitz, who in turn talked to his friend, the governor's counsel, and got his support. A contrite, remorse-stricken Dennis Levecque, pathetically eager to undo the damage he perceived he had done, talked his friends in the labor movement into supporting Zimmerman's nomination; his compelling argument was the almost certain loss of the governorship to the Republicans should the civil rights job to go anyone but a distinguished and neutral outsider.

But the decisive move was sending Dean Meyeroff to talk to his brothers-in-law, the Kesslers. When Bobbie Kessler, that year chairman of the State Chamber of Commerce, telephoned Tim Doyle to tell him that Judge Rosenbaum had withdrawn his candidacy and that the business community of Capital City would support Heinz Zimmerman and no one else, the battle was won.

Or almost won. As Sister Renée had predicted, Tim Doyle refused to have the governor offer the job unless Zimmerman would declare his acceptance beforehand. And no one, of course, had even mentioned the job to Zimmerman, let alone obtained his consent. But who could talk to Heinz Zimmerman and persuade him to take the offer?

There was only one person who had a chance to be listened to: Erwin Ritter.

It took a whole morning to persuade him to take on the mission. Then Ritter disappeared into the president's office and they all waited endlessly, saying nothing, in Ritter's conference room. What happened between the two no one was ever told. Ritter was gone for two hours or more.

When he reappeared, he looked a very old man, said simply, "He'll take it," and vanished into his office, firmly closing the door behind him.

It took another week to work out all the details. But the following Monday morning the *Capital City Gazette* carried on its front page a four-column article:

At a hastily called press conference last night Governor Willie Ewing announced the appointment of Father Heinz Zimmerman to a five-year term as Chairman of the state's Civil Rights Commission. Father Zimmerman, 56, has been President of Capital City's St. Jerome University for almost twenty years. He will be sworn in as Chairman of the Civil Rights Commission on April 15, with Bishop O'Malley of the Roman Catholic Diocese of Capital City administering the oath of office.

"I know of no one more qualified to fill this important position than Heinz Zimmerman," Governor Ewing said. "He is one of our nation's most distinguished educators and one of the state's most distinguished citizens. He has served the cause of civil rights with great distinction on a Presidential Civil Rights Commission. And he has the full support of all groups in the state."

Father Zimmerman's appointment is indeed being widely applauded. "We have full confidence in Heinz Zimmerman, his objectivity, his knowledge, and his humanity," declared Mr. Ralph Christenberry, state director of the AFL-CIO and chairman of Capital City's Black Caucus. "An outstanding Christian and a fine choice," was the comment of Rev. George Hammond of Park Avenue Congregational Church and chairman of the City's Ministerial Council. "This appointment should satisfy everyone," declared Professor Carlos Fernandez of Buffalo Junction State College and state director of *La Causa*. "The state can be congratulated on this appointment," we were told by Mr. Robert Kessler, chairman of the State Chamber of Commerce; "we are fortunate indeed to have so distinguished a man in our midst."

The state's Civil Rights Commission was created by former Governor Colebrook in 1975. Its first chairman was the Rev. Thomas Langley Gould, whose sudden death a few weeks ago created the vacancy Father Zimmerman has now been appointed to fill. The job pays $62,500 a year.

And on the front page of the paper's second part with the local news there was another banner headline, with an even longer article:

St. Jerome University announces that its long-time President, Father Heinz Zimmerman, has resigned, effective immediately, to accept appointment as Chairman of the State's Civil Rights Commission (see also front-page story).

"We are unhappy," the chairman of the university's Board of Regents, Mr. Jack Mulcahey, declared, "to lose Heinz Zimmerman. He has made St. Jerome University what it is today. But we realize that our claims must take a back seat to those of public office. And we are proud that Heinz Zimmerman has been selected to fill so important a position."

Father Zimmerman has been on the St. Jerome faculty since 1952, when he received his doctorate in Logic from Freiburg University in Germany. He became the university's Acting President in 1960 and its President two years later, in 1962. Under his leadership St. Jerome University has grown from a student body of fewer than 2,500 to 12,000 students today, has gone fully co-educational, has increased its faculty from 120 to almost 1,000 members and its endowment from $4.5 to $59 million. When Father Zimmerman took over as Acting President, St. Jerome University had a Law School and an Undergraduate School of Business in addition to the Undergraduate College of Arts and Sciences. It now has a full Graduate School of Arts and Sciences offering masters and doctors degrees in all academic disciplines; a Graduate School of Management; a fully accredited Engineering School offering both a bachelor's and a master's degree; and professional schools in Nursing, Dentistry, and Pharmacy. It has achieved national stature and is considered to be on a par with leading research universities such as Chicago, Yale, and Stanford.

Father Zimmerman's achievements have been recognized by many honors and awards, including honorary doctorates from Columbia University in New York City and from Notre Dame University. He has twice been featured on the cover of *Time* magazine.

Pending selection of a new President, Father Erwin Ritter, 63, has been appointed Acting President. Father Ritter has been Dean, Executive Dean, and Chief Academic Officer of St. Jerome University since 1954. He has agreed to serve as Acting President to the end of the current calendar year. "I am convinced," he told our reporter, "that we will have selected a new President by Christmas.

The Board of Regents has already appointed a search committee headed by Mr. Jack Mulcahey, the board's chairman. We shall look both inside and outside the university and at both lay people and religious. We already have several very promising candidates in mind."

In a related action, Mr. Jack Mulcahey, the university's board chairman, announced that he was making a donation in the amount of $1.5 million to establish a Heinz Zimmerman Distinguished University Professorship in Philosophy at St. Jerome University. At Father Zimmerman's request, Acting President Erwin Ritter has agreed to become the first occupant of the new chair upon stepping down as the university's Acting President at the end of 1980.

"Do you believe me now, Martin?" Lisa Holloway asked her husband when he came dashing into her bedroom, woke her up, and excitedly showed her the announcement of Heinz Zimmerman's resignation as president of St. Jerome University in the *Capital City Gazette* he had just picked up outside the door. "I told you I'd make them pay."

"And don't tell me again," she continued, "that I was unfair to him. You didn't believe me that he knew we were being persecuted by a Godless, anti-Catholic conspiracy. But if he hadn't had a guilty conscience he wouldn't have made that telephone call to Harriet Beecher Stowe to get a teaching job for you. That proved he knew that he should have reappointed you and was just too much of a coward to do it.

"You were appalled when I said aloud that the relationship with Agnes Muller is a scandal and immoral. Remember, you told me it wasn't true? But do you really think they would have panicked the way they did if there hadn't been something to it? When they immediately put a typist into the office where those two had been together so cozily, I knew I was right. If they'd been innocent, they wouldn't have done that.

"Well, at least I've spoilt their fun and games and brought a little truth and decency into the stinking mess that's St. Jerome."

"Yes," said her husband meekly, "I admit you were right and I was wrong. Thank God it's over."

"But, Lisa," and he suddenly grew animated, "I have wonderful news! You know how depressed I've been about not landing a job yet for next fall. My résumé has gone to every Catholic college in the country and we didn't even get a single nibble. And the St. Jerome checks will stop coming in three months.

"Last night after you'd gone to bed, Boglund called. He's lined up a job as senior scientist in the testing lab of a big pharmaceutical company in Chicago. I'll get a formal offer within a day or two—and the job pays more than twice what I've been getting as assistant professor."

"*Martin Holloway*," she screamed, "you must know I'll leave you the moment you take a job in industry! I won't live with a man who helps capitalist swine make filthy profits out of poor people's sickness. You were nothing but a tool of those exploiters when I first met you, and a heathen to boot. You go back to your vomit like a dog. I won't follow you!"

"Lisa, Lisa," he groaned, and tried to take her hand in his, only to have it snatched back when he touched it, "you know I need you. You know I love you. I realize how much I owe you—how you led me from my wasted, Godless life to the true faith and into the true Church, and how you slaved for me for four years typing in that dreary office so I could give up my job and go back to graduate school.

"But, Lisa, I've told you often enough that capitalists and capitalism had nothing to do with my work in industry. No matter what the system or who runs it, somebody has to do what I was doing—and I did it better, I daresay, than I've done my teaching. Whoever does the job, wherever it's done, it's got to be done the same way: make sure that the water is pure and the ingredients uncontaminated, that the right yeast strains go into the fermentation tanks and the drugs that come out are pure and potent. I wasn't exploited, no matter who else might have been. I was paid well and treated right."

"Martin Holloway, I forbid you to talk such drivel," Lisa said, sitting bolt upright in bed. "You are not going back to industry—not as long as I'm alive.

"But don't worry, Martin," she added in a quieter voice. "I have it all worked out. Remember the Catholic Commune in the New Mexico mountains, the one I told you about where I lived for two years in the late sixties before I went back to Cleveland to finish college and met you? I've written to the priest who runs it. He's forgiven me for leaving ten years ago and is willing to take me back and have you join—there are still a few people left there. It's going to be hard work; we try to raise all our own food. But we lead a Christian life like the early followers of Jesus. And at least we'll have the one hundred and sixty dollars a month extra from the trust fund my father set up when I first went off to college. I wrote Father Joseph to expect us around the first of June."

Holloway started to say something. Then he looked at his wife's face and thought better of it.

Agnes Muller was sitting at her desk on which lay a copy of the *Capital City Gazette*, with her head buried in her arms and sobbing, when Heinz Zimmerman arrived at the office that Monday morning. She did not even look up when he came in and wished her good morning, nor did she return his greeting. "Agnes," he cried, thoroughly alarmed, "what is the matter? We've known of my leaving for a week, there's nothing new. Why has the announcement upset you?"

And when she did not respond, he said: "I didn't want to talk to you about it until my appointment had become official. But Agnes, my dear, I count on you to continue as my partner in the new assignment. I plan to appoint you the Commission's staff director the day I take office—I've already cleared it with John Lindstrom, the governor's counsel."

"No, Heinz," she muttered in a weak voice. "No, please, no.

"Heinz, please don't scold me, I couldn't take it. But Erwin Ritter came to my house yesterday and I accepted his offer to become vice president of Administration and Budgets for St. Jerome. He's going to appoint Sister Mary Annunciata from the Women's Campus to work under me as my assistant and the university's budget director. I didn't want to take it— all I want is to get away from St. Jerome and Capital City as fast and as far as I can. But Erwin pleaded with me to stay and help him preserve what you've built here and to continue your work.

"Oh, Heinz," she wailed, "I didn't want to say yes, but what else could I do?"—and she buried her face in her arms again and began to cry wildly.

"Don't desert me, Agnes, please. Agnes, I need you." He put his hands in a tender gesture on her shoulders and awkwardly, clumsily tried to caress them.

But she shook his hands off, almost violently.

"Don't touch me. Don't touch me!" Her voice rose to a pitch of hysteria. "It's too late." But she calmed down right away. "Don't worry about me, Heinz," she said. "I'm used to being a widow."

A mulish look, the look of a pouting ten-year-old, came over Heinz Zimmerman's face. Wordlessly, he left Agnes, walked through the door into his office, and began to take down the honorary doctorates from his trophy wall.

"I'll leave on a three-week vacation until I'm sworn in on the new job," he said aloud, as if talking to no one in particular.

At this moment, his telephone rang. He hesitated a second. But Agnes made no move to pick it up, so he answered it himself.

It was Seymour Bercovitz.

"Heinz," he said, "I'm calling to give you my very, very best wishes for the new job. I suspect you consider it a comedown. But you'll find you are wrong. The job was just waiting for someone like you, someone courageous and dynamic and imaginative, to become a key position in the state. You're just the man for it.

"And, Heinz, I'm calling to convey an invitation from my two children—and I concur in it wholeheartedly. You know we have a much bigger house than the three of us can use. Years ago we converted the top floor into a separate apartment—three rooms, kitchen and bath, with its own entrance from the street. We thought we might rent it out but we never did. It's fully furnished. The kids and I should be honored and delighted if you were to move in as our guest and stay as long as you want to—at least until you've found a permanent place to live.

"But," Seymour went on, and his voice dropped a whole octave to become a whisper, "that's not really what I'm calling about. I know, Heinz, you have other things on your mind, but I would be immensely grateful if I could have a few minutes of your time to tell you something personal. I have to talk to you about it. May I?"

When Zimmerman still remained silent, Bercovitz continued:

"Do you remember, Heinz, my telling you a few months ago why I dropped out of the seminary when I lost my faith in God? I still haven't regained it. But now, after what has happened at St. Jerome, I know that there is evil. No, I don't mean that wretched creature, that woman, who started it all. She is only sick—and I still expect medicine to find a cure for her disease, or at least a treatment that makes the likes of her realize that they are deluded. I mean all the others, the sane and normal ones, with their pettiness, their meanness, their delight in inflicting pain, their hurt vanities and inflated egos and their cowardice. Now I know that there really is evil—and then one needs God."

Seymour had become agitated; his voice had risen and he was talking so fast he almost slurred his words. When he stopped, Zimmerman could hear him taking a few deep breaths.

He continued at last in quite a different voice, low-pitched, and so slowly that it sounded almost like a chant:

"What I called to tell you, Heinz, is that I went on Friday to Father Neeley at St. Anne's and asked him to give me instruction in the Catholic faith. I don't know whether I can regain faith, but I do know I need it."

"We have betrayed him," said Bishop O'Malley, when Tom Martini brought in the morning paper with its news of Zimmerman's appointment as chairman of the State Civil Rights Commission and of his resignation from the presidency of St. Jerome University. "We have thrown a good and decent priest to the wolves."

"With due respect, Bishop," said Martini, "I disagree. We have saved Father Zimmerman. He made himself hopelessly vulnerable when he couldn't resist the temptation to do good and put through that impetuous telephone call to Harriet Beecher Stowe. And then all the tensions, all the conflicts, all the contradictions you saw so clearly when this sordid business first started with that poisonous letter from that wretched woman, all of them came out into the open. Every one of them was petty and mean and despicable. But the real issue is not. And it's the real issue that has defeated Father Zimmerman—and you and me. What we've been able to do not only saves Father Zimmerman and gives him a new sphere of contribution and effectiveness. It also gives St. Jerome University the breathng space it needs to straighten itself out."

"Quite a speech, Tom," said the bishop, and he made a little mock bow. "I bet you practiced it before you came in here today."

"That isn't quite fair, sir," protested Martini. "The university is going all out to honor Father Zimmerman. There's the Distinguished University Professorship in his name Mr. Mulcahey is endowing. The Administration Building is going to be renamed Zimmerman Hall. And—though

Father Zimmerman isn't supposed to know it yet—he'll be given an honorary doctorate at the June Commencement."

"That's making it up to the victim of judicial murder by giving him a first-class funeral," growled the bishop.

"Don't get me wrong," he continued in a milder tone. "I do not criticize you—quite the contrary. You pulled off a near-miracle, I admit; and I've already told Bernie Murtagh how much I admire what the two of you worked out. You sure got St. Jerome off the hook on which they were trying so hard to hang themselves. Of course, it doesn't solve the problem Zimmerman wanted to ignore—how St. Jerome can be both a great and a Catholic university. I don't envy Heinz Zimmerman's successor; no matter how good a man he is, he won't last three years. Either Willy Huber or the faculty or the two together will kill him off. But, then, that wasn't your problem and it isn't ours. What you did was a virtuoso performance. I haven't seen a better one and I'm full of genuine admiration.

"But that doesn't alter the fact that we betrayed a good man and a fellow priest whose only fault was that he exercised a little Christian compassion. Instead of defending him against libel, slander, and petty intrigue, we took his life's work away from him and kicked him upstairs into a meaningless non-job where he won't have anything to do except listen to the complaint of a black cop that he should have been given fifty extra points in the sergeant's exam because his grandpappy was a slave."

Tom Martini was still wondering how he should answer the bishop—indeed, whether he should answer at all—when the telephone rang.

"It's Monsignor Allessandri from Washington," Tom said, as he handed the receiver over. "He wants to speak to you in private," and Martini got up and left the room.

"Good morning, Patrick," said the familiar voice in its beautiful Oxford English with the almost imperceptible trace of an Italian accent. "I hope I'm not disturbing you, but I do need ten minutes of your time. What I have to say shouldn't wait, especially as it's all good news.

"First, I have been instructed by His Excellency the Nuncio to call the American bishops with whom I've worked and tell them that I have been called back to Rome. I shall leave here by the end of the week. I have been appointed Papal Nuncio to Colombia and will be raised to Bishop before Easter. I am supposed to take over in Bogotá by early July. And I need a few weeks to be briefed, to brush up on my Spanish—it's been almost fifteen years since I last used it in my first diplomatic assignment as a junior secretary at the Nunciatura in Buenos Aires—and to learn what 'Liberation Theology' is all about.

"And so let me say thanks for all your cooperation during my four years in your country. I can't tell you how much I appreciate your friendship and your many kindnesses to me. I am particularly grateful to you for what you taught me about organization, management, and developing people. I shall consider myself your student and in your debt the rest of my career. No, Patrick, I really mean it.

"And now," Allessandri continued, "I have a second, more important message for you from His Excellency. He just read in the Washington morning papers how superbly you handled that awkward affair at St. Jerome University. Don't protest— who else but you and that young Father Martini of yours could have found so elegant and perfect a solution? My congratulations, and His Excellency asked me to add his thanks. You have averted what could have become a damaging scandal and have done so by advancing and strengthening the moral position of the Church, and moving a prominent and widely respected priest into a visible leadership position in public service. '*Bravissimo,*' that's what His Excellency said when he read the news, and you know he is not the enthusiastic type."

There was a pause—Allessandri, O'Malley thought, was

consulting his notes again—then he continued:

"I haven't forgotten our talk about your secretary, Father Martini, and his future, nor your telling me that you had entrusted the St. Jerome problem to him. And I must admit the way he worked it out fully justifies all you told me about his being an extraordinary young man. So I am delighted to be able to tell you that the Nuncio has accepted your recommendation. As soon as you telephone me that Father Martini will accept, the Nuncio will announce his appointment as American attaché at the Washington Nunciatura. It's usually a three-year appointment, as you know. Afterwards Martini should be able to choose between joining the papal diplomatic service permanently or moving over to the National Conference of Catholic Bishops as an associate secretary. I am only sorry I won't be here when he reports for duty. But I do expect you to phone me his acceptance right away—today, I hope. I want to call him myself before I leave to congratulate him."

O'Malley was overwhelmed and started to say so, but Allessandri cut him off.

"One moment, Patrick," he said; "I'm not quite finished. I have kept the best news for the end.

"It gives me exquisite pleasure to inform you on the instructions of His Excellency the Nuncio that the Holy Father has acceded to your petition and will raise Capital City to an archbishopric and establish within the archdiocese a new bishopric and diocese at Palmer. His Excellency has charged me to convey the Holy Father's hope that you will accept elevation to Archbishop and serve in Capital City until you reach retirement age, if the good Lord preserves you in life and health until then, as all of us hope and pray. May I be the first to congratulate you, and to say how delighted I am that my period of service in the United States concludes with such a happy, such a blessed event?

"I know, Patrick, you suggested that Monsignor Sullivan be put into Palmer. Frankly, His Excellency the Nuncio feels—

and Rome agrees—that a new diocese needs a younger man, who can stay in the post a good many years. The Holy Father has therefore decided to raise your Vicar General Monsignor Corrigan to the rank and title of Bishop of Palmer, and to appoint Monsignor Sullivan to become your auxiliary bishop in Capital City. You are overloaded and need help, especially with ceremonial duties.

"The Holy Father will announce these appointments in the week after Easter—the date set is April 10. You will then be asked to come to Rome as soon as possible, no later than the first week in May, to receive the Archbishop's pallium. Corrigan and Sullivan will be asked to accompany you and to be consecrated at the same time. This means that I'll be seeing you soon—I'll plan to be in Rome then. Rome further suggests that you plan your formal enthronement in Capital City to take place on the Feast Day of Saints Peter and Paul—June 29. May I be so presumptuous as to invite myself to the great occasion? I have to be in Bogotá around July 3 or 4 and can easily make the detour to Capital City. And the following Sunday, Rome suggests, you formally install your two new bishops.

"Again let me say," Allessandri added with a flourish, "how happy I am that I can finish my American tour of duty by bringing such good news to a dear friend, and how delighted I am that I don't have to say 'Goodbye' but 'arrividerci.' And don't forget, please, we'd like to get Father Martini's acceptance as soon as possible. Do you think you can phone it in today?"

"I am overwhelmed and more than grateful, sir," Tom Martini responded when Bishop O'Malley gave him Monsignor Allessandri's message a few minutes later. The Bishop saw that the young priest had tears in his eyes and was close to choking on his emotions. "I know this is the most fabulous and most exciting opportunity that will ever come my way.

"But, Bishop," Martini continued, "when Monsignor Allessandri called, I was just about to tell you of my own plans and to make a request. My term as your secretary is about ended; I know your four-year rule and I've been here more than three and a half years already. Of course I never dreamed of anything so grand as the Washington assignment you got for me. Don't protest, sir; *you* were the one that procured it. I thought you might offer me a position as a department head under a vice chancellor here in the diocese or at most a vice chancellorship.

"But, sir—and I do hope you can forgive me—I have decided to ask you respectfully to relieve me of my administrative and executive duties, and to assign me instead to where I can minister to individuals—to a parish or as chaplain to a prison or a hospital—though I hope you won't make me a chaplain at a university and a faculty member right now. I hope you don't think me ungrateful. I know I could never hope for a kinder boss or for one from whom I could learn more. But I'm determined to become a pastor and stop being an executive."

"When did you reach this decision, Tom?" asked O'Malley in a very soft voice.

"I started thinking about it a few months ago when I realized that my four years as your secretary would soon be up. But what really made up my mind was our first talk about Father Zimmerman. Do you remember, Bishop, what you said about people who don't know that they are ambitious and how endangered they are, that morning when Mrs. Holloway's letter arrived?"

"But, Tom," the startled bishop protested, "I didn't mean you."

"I realize that, sir. I know that you'd be direct if you wanted to talk *about* me. Still, you talked *to* me, whether you meant to or not. It was quite a shock, I must say. But I needed it; and I'm grateful."

"You realize, Tom," the bishop said—and now his voice was stern—"that your going into parish work would be a wicked waste of your gifts. You are so very good as an administrator and executive, and so few are. There are dozens who can do a decent job in a parish or as chaplain. If ever I saw anybody with a true vocation for being an executive, it's you."

"I'm deeply grateful for your praise, sir, and flattered. But it's just because I'm good at it that I want to leave while I still can. I enjoy it too much. I know that if I don't get out now, I never will. And it's not what I went into the Church for."

There was a pause. Then, "Very well, Tom," said the bishop. "Of course, you've earned the right to go where you think you belong, although both Allessandri and I will be very disappointed. But you are making a serious mistake. Tell me, have you given any thought to where you'll be if it doesn't work out, if you find that your vocation is not pastoral work and being a parish priest? I hope I'm wrong; but, Tom, I'm almost sure that in a few months you'll be bored stiff and find the life humdrum and pretty frustrating. You're used to so much bigger a world than the four walls of a parish."

"I wouldn't be surprised, sir, if you're right, although I hope you aren't. But I'm determined to find out. I'll give myself two years. If after two years I find that my vocation is not to be a pastor but to be an executive, I still wouldn't want to be an executive in the Church.

"I would want to stay a priest, I believe, but I'd look for my career elsewhere than in the Church. I don't think I've ever told you, sir, that my parents have been quite successful in their business. They've built up the small neighborhood grocery store my dad inherited when he came back from the service in World War II into a profitable chain: five Italian supermarkets in and around Capital City—they're called 'Alberto's'—and each has a trattoria attached to it that serves Italian meals, and a gift shop. My father always wanted me to come into the business and was very disappointed when I went into the seminary instead of going to Business School. If I don't make it as a pastor, I'd rather go in as an executive with my father. I am sure I could build the family business into a national chain; all right, it won't be another McDonald's or Kentucky Fried Chicken—but in ten years it should be a sizable company. Alberto's has the right formula. What it needs is management—and that, sir, you have taught me.

"With all due respect for you and your great office, if I have to be an executive, I see more scope and a greater contribution for me in a business than in the Church. Here it's all rules and regulations and paperwork. The main task is to preserve, to prevent change, discourage innovation, and not go in for experiments. To do reasonably well what has been done so much better many times before. And most of the administrative work is so petty. Do you realize, sir, how much of your time and energy goes into taking care of alcoholic priests? And then the politics! No, Your Excellency, if the Lord has meant me to be an executive, it's not in the Church, no matter how much I love it.

"So, please convey my gratitude to Monsignor Allessandri and accept my thanks for all you've been doing for me and have tried to do for me. I know how much I owe you. Tell Monsignor Allessandri, please, that I am most sensible of the honor. It's very tempting. But I am determined to resist the temptation."

"Tom is wrong," Bishop O'Malley thought after the young man had left. "Doesn't he realize that the parish priest and the prison chaplain can do their job only because there's someone who sits where I sit taking care of the paperwork and worrying about alcoholic priests and petty politics and teaching people and developing and placing them? He'll be in for one heck of a surprise if he thinks there's no routine and no politics and no worryng about alcoholic or dishonest store managers in running Alberto's. It's quite unthinkable to me that he can turn down the Washington offer—it's tailor-made for him, and there's so much good he could do in the job. But perhaps, after what he's just seen at St. Jerome, it's understandable that he wants to resist the temptation to do good.

"But what about myself?" Bishop O'Malley asked himself suddenly. And such a wave of black despair rose in him that he had to steady his head with his hands to fight the nausea and dizziness. "I have failed in my duty as bishop, failed miserably. Of course the Order of St. Jerome and its university are outside my jurisdiction. But I am the diocesan and the guardian of Faith and Morals in my diocese. And if what happened at St. Jerome was not gross, flagrant immorality, I wouldn't know what is. What they normally mean, of course, when they talk of immorality are the sins of the flesh. But the sins of the spirit are as much or more immoral: the sins of pride and envy and of bearing false witness against one's neighbor. I've not fought against them but have given in to them and sacrificed a good man, a good Christian and a fellow priest, to avoid controversy, unpleasantness, criticism from the Nuncio, and adverse publicity. And instead of being punished for my failure, I am being praised and rewarded by being made Archbishop.

"Of course, I could refuse and retire. I am sixty-three years old, after all." But the bishop knew that he would not refuse and would not retire.

"To be sure," he said to himself, "I can always tell myself that it's the right thing to do. Capital City should have been an archbishopric years ago. I can tell myself that I'm doing it for my clergy, and for the faithful in the diocese to whom the news will bring such joy and pride. It's true, but not true enough. I know I want it—and what's worse, I know I'll enjoy it."